'Why didn't you tell Philip it was all over, that you were going to be my wife?' Sander demanded.

She took a deep, steadying breath. 'You can't be serious about tying yourself to a woman you obviously despise, just for your cousin's sake!'

'It isn't solely for Rhoda's sake. I need a wife.' He offered Mia a sandwich before continuing, 'The Davison Lazenby Merchant Bank was founded in the early 1900s by my grandfather. The old man was a diehard; so was my father. Before I can take my father's place as head of the bank, under the terms of his will I have to be respectably married.'

Cynically he went on, 'There are plenty of beautiful women about, but, as far as I'm concerned, a lovely face is no compensation for an empty head. Though your morals leave quite a lot to be desired, you have the combination of brains and beauty I've been looking for. Treated with a firm hand, you should fit the bill nicely...'

MILLS & BOON LIMITED
ETON HOUSE · 18-24 PARADISE ROAD
RICHMOND · SURREY · TW9 1SR

HONG KONG HONEYMOON

BY
LEE WILKINSON

MILLS & BOON LIMITED
ETON HOUSE   18-24 PARADISE ROAD
RICHMOND   SURREY   TW9 1SR

*First published in Great Britain 1991
by Mills & Boon Limited*

© Lee Wilkinson 1991

*Australian copyright 1991
Philippine copyright 1991
This edition 1991*

ISBN 0 263 77299 3

*Set in Times Roman 10½ on 11¼ pt.
01-9111-52434 C*

Made and printed in Great Britain

CHAPTER ONE

RHODA'S birthday party was in full swing when Mia arrived at the Rayburns' country mansion. Having thanked Michael Brent, Rayfield's export manager, and his wife Sue, who had offered her a lift from town, she accepted a glass of champagne from a hovering waiter and headed for the ballroom.

She was wearing a grey chiffon dress with full sleeves and a circular skirt that swirled gently around her slender legs. A dull gold belt was its only ornamentation. With it she had teamed grey kid sandals and a small squashy bag with a gold chain handle.

Tall and slim, her ash-blonde hair curling softly on to her shoulders, she made her way with an easy, natural grace between talking, laughing groups, occasionally pausing to have a word with someone she knew.

Outwardly smiling and carefree, inwardly she was wrought-up and tense. The situation being what it was, she hadn't wanted to come tonight. All she'd wanted was for the party to be over and done with, and Philip to be free.

And there was an additional reason for her reluctance. Sander Davison would almost certainly be here. She wished, not for the first time, that Rhoda's cousin had stayed over half a world away in Hong Kong.

Knowing he was quite a bit older than Rhoda, and a wealthy banker, Mia had imagined him to be middle-aged and dull with receding hair and an incipient paunch. On meeting him she'd discovered he was the very antithesis of her preconceived idea.

She recalled only too clearly the first time he'd walked into her office. Janet, her secretary, had looked up from opening the morning mail and fairly goggled. Mia had felt a quiver run through her, an odd, unexpected, unexplainable surge of raw antagonism.

He was six feet three or four, wide across the shoulders, and handsome as the devil himself, with an arrogant tilt to his dark head. She had found herself staring at his mouth, a mouth that made a series of prickly sensations chase each other across her suddenly heated skin.

Instantly, instinctively, she had made up her mind to let Janet deal with this disquieting stranger.

She had been bending assiduously over the papers she was currently working on, when two palms had slapped down on her desk. Startled, she had looked up and found his darkly attractive face only inches from her own. His skin, she had noted, was healthily tanned, his long-lashed eyes green as jade beneath curving brows.

'My name is Sander Davison,' he'd informed her pleasantly, while the diamond edge to his tone gave notice that he had no intention of being deliberately ignored.

'Sander Davison,' she'd repeated, and found herself thinking that he looked more like some conquistador of old than a merchant banker.

Just then Philip had appeared and apologised profusely for keeping him waiting. As he was led into the inner sanctum, the banker had turned and given Mia an ironic little smile.

At that, and every subsequent encounter, he'd challenged her, destroying her calm and throwing her into a state of confusion.

He was altogether too clever, with a mind as sharp as a samurai sword, too dominant, too sure of his effect on women, she thought waspishly, for her taste.

Whenever they met, a flame ignited in his cool green eyes, his look a kind of mental seduction as though he was making love to her in his mind. Hating the turbulent effect he had on her, the way her body filled with heat and her composure melted away, Mia always tried her hardest to avoid him.

But when she'd attempted to excuse herself from tonight's party, her father had looked up from the papers littering his desk and said shortly, 'Don't be a fool, girl, of course you must go.'

Mia had wavered. Even over comparatively small things, James Fielding's temper could be explosive if he was crossed, and after his recent heart attack she was afraid of sending his blood-pressure soaring to a dangerous level.

'Rhoda would be hurt if you didn't,' he had added, as though that clinched the matter.

Relieved, more likely, Mia thought. Though putting on a good show in front of people, in private Rhoda couldn't be bothered to disguise her animosity.

Now, wishing she'd stuck to her guns, Mia looked around the crowded room, hoping to catch a reassuring glimpse of Philip. But she was disappointed; he was nowhere to be seen.

Then, quite close, she noticed Jacqueline May, a stunningly dressed woman with eyes as blue as sapphires and frizzy black hair, whose beautiful, striking face regularly adorned the covers of glossy fashion magazines.

Mia, with fair hair, grey eyes, and a pale, clear skin, had always thought of herself as nondescript. Now she sighed a little, feeling like a bleached watercolour compared to a vivid oil-painting.

A burly man who had been partially blocking her view moved away, and she saw that by the model's side was Sander Davison, looking devastatingly attractive in impeccable evening clothes.

Watching him warily through long, gold-tipped lashes, Mia began to edge away, feeling her usual need to run for cover, to hide and only emerge when he was gone and the danger was past.

Suddenly a plump, over-dressed woman bumped her elbow, almost spilling the champagne, and paused to apologise.

Mia smiled and assured her, 'It's quite all right, really. There's no harm done.'

The smile still hovering on her lips, she looked up incautiously, and met Sander Davison's brilliant gaze. Some glances were like collisions. This had the same impact as walking into a plate-glass window.

Her heart lurching with shock, she let her eyes slide past him, and hurriedly slipped away to lose herself in the throng.

Rhoda, a petite redhead, with a round face and sherry-coloured eyes, was over by the bar, standing between her own father and Mia's.

William Rayburn and James Fielding were lifelong friends and business partners, jointly owning Rayfield Pharmaceuticals.

Seeing her father smile indulgently at Rhoda, Mia stifled a pang. Since early childhood she had done her utmost to please him, to try to win his love and approval, but it was William's daughter who had always held pride of place in his affections.

A group had started to play, and a lot of the younger crowd were dancing. The music was loud, with a strong, rhythmic beat.

Though the french windows were flung wide the room seemed overheated, stuffy, and a gradual buildup of tension had left Mia with the beginnings of a splitting headache.

There was still no sign of Philip.

Grey eyes cloudy, she placed her glass on a trolley standing by the wall, and thankfully escaped into the fresh evening air.

Wending her way the length of the flagged terrace, where just a few couples were sitting or strolling, she descended the steps at the far end. It was quiet and blessedly dark beyond the range of the fairy lanterns strung between the trees. Her thoughts on Philip, she followed the path to a tiny, secluded arbour.

Intelligent and ambitious, Philip Measham was Rayfield's sales director. He was tall, fair-haired, and very good-looking, with an engaging boyish charm. Mia had been his personal assistant for over a year, and for almost the same length of time had worshipped him in secret.

Putting down her evening bag, she rested her arms on the flat stone parapet and gazed over the sunken garden. Though it was only the end of March, it was warm as a summer night. A slight breeze fluttered the long sleeves of her dress, lifted the silken weight of her hair and detached a tendril that caressed her cheek with a lover's touch. She sighed.

At this very spot on a mild day last Christmas, after leaving the house-party to take a stroll through the garden, Philip had kissed her and admitted that *he* loved *her*.

Caught up in the wonder of it, overwhelmed by joy and an almost fierce gratitude, Mia had run her fingers into his fine blond hair and kissed him back with a recklessness that had shaken them both.

Only later had come the guilt. Philip was Rhoda's fiancé, and had been for some months.

Weeks of bittersweet happiness, of longing and uncertainty, had followed. They had met in secret; brief, snatched moments that satisfied neither of them.

But after tonight all that would be changed. His pale blue eyes intense, Philip had promised, 'As soon as this blasted party's over I'm going to tell Rhoda I want to end the engagement.'

'What if it affects your prospects with the firm?' Mia had suggested worriedly.

For a moment a frown had creased his forehead, then it had smoothed away and he had said decisively, 'That's a risk I'm going to have to take. I can't go on like this any longer.'

So soon he would be free. Free, after a decent interval, to court her openly and make her his wife . . .

The brush of an approaching footfall broke into her reverie, and she knew with a surge of gladness that he had come to find her.

Turning, she discovered he was close behind her. With a whispered, 'Oh, darling!' she went into his arms and lifted her face for his kiss.

Steely arms had closed around her and a mouth was claiming hers before Mia realised with a jolt that it *wasn't* Philip. This man was too tall, too broad, altogether too muscular. And Philip, though ardent, was gentle and considerate. He never held her, never kissed her, in this passionate, masterful way.

Stiffening, she tried to pull free, her hands pressing against broad shoulders. But the arms holding her only tightened and the mouth became even more demanding, deepening the kiss until her senses started to whirl.

A hand, warm and electrifying through the gauzy material of her dress, started to follow her slender curves. Her breath quickened and a longing, hot as molten lava, began to flow through her bloodstream.

Though she had fought to repress them, she had all the normal urges of a healthy young woman, and only her keen sense of wrongdoing, of guilt towards Rhoda, had kept her from giving in to Philip's pleas that they should become lovers. Now a sexual hunger too long suppressed and denied flared into life, demanding to be satisfied.

Desire killed reason, and all attempt at resistance ended. Her arms went around the strong neck and her soft body melted fluidly against the hard male one.

Her mind was so clouded with passion that she raised no objection when skilful fingers drew down the fine zip at the back of her dress and pushed the grey chiffon away from her shoulders.

Those compelling lips left hers and roamed over the expanse of satin-smooth skin. A tongue-tip touched and tasted the hollow at the base of her throat, then moved to the cleft between her breasts. She was on fire, burning, conscious only of the wild pleasure that seeking mouth was giving...

Footsteps, and a woman's shrill laugh, were like a shower of icy water. But, before Mia could even begin to collect her scattered wits, deft hands rearranged and re-zipped her dress and she was turned so that the tall figure shielded her from any prying eyes.

As soon as the sauntering pair had passed, Mia pulled herself out of her companion's light hold and swung to face him. Though she could make out little more than the white of his shirt front, and the gleam of his eyes, she knew who it was. Perhaps subconsciously she had known from the start.

Angry and agitated, her heart racing so fast she felt giddy, she demanded, 'How dare you?'

Sander Davison's soft chuckle told her he was lazily amused.

'You sound for all the world like a Victorian heroine,' he derided her. 'Though I have to admit you certainly didn't *act* like one!'

Mia was glad the darkness hid her flaming cheeks.

'In fact,' he went on quizzically, 'it was something of a surprise to find you responding to me quite so passionately.'

She gritted her teeth. 'I didn't know it *was* you.'

He pounced. 'Then who did you think it was? Who were you waiting for?'

'I wasn't waiting for anyone,' she denied huskily.

'Do you usually whisper "darling" and throw yourself into the arms of just any man who happens to come along?'

Refusing to answer, she tried to brush past him, but his fingers closed around her upper arm as if they were a steel fetter, not hurting, but keeping her exactly where he wanted her to be.

'Don't rush off,' he drawled. 'I left the party especially to talk to you.'

'How did you know where I was?' she demanded.

'I followed you on to the terrace, and you led me here.'

Mia looked down her small, straight nose. 'I didn't even notice you.'

'Pretending not to notice me seems to be a habit of yours. A habit I don't much care for,' he added silkily. 'So I hope it's one you're now cured of.'

'Oh, I'm cured all right,' she said bitterly. 'Though I may well develop another one.'

His voice edged with laughter, he suggested, 'Such as throwing yourself into my arms every time you feel frustrated?'

'Such as turning tail and running!'

'You do that already,' he pointed out wickedly.

'And, for your information, I am *not* frustrated,' she hurried on, ignoring his taunt. 'Now, if you wouldn't mind?' She jerked her imprisoned arm.

'You certainly acted as if you were,' he insisted, disregarding her attempt to break loose. 'I've got an excellent cure for frustration,' he went on softly. Then at the sound of approaching feet he sighed. 'It's a shade too public here, but if you'd like——'

'I'd like you to let go of me,' she broke in heatedly. 'If you don't, I'll scream!'

'How melodramatic!'

Ignoring his mockery, she rushed on, 'You'll have some explaining to do to your girlfriend if I cause a scene.'

'But you wouldn't do that.'

He was right, damn him. She'd always hated to make a spectacle of herself.

A young couple appeared, walking slowly, heads close together, arms entwined, totally wrapped up in each other.

As he turned to look at the pair his grip slackened a trifle. Pulling herself free, Mia hurried past them, almost breaking into a run in her eagerness to get away. The nerve of the man! she fumed. Following her and... Well, she had been partly to blame, honesty made her admit. No, *more* than partly.

Oh, dear God, how had Sander Davison been able to make her forget all her repressions and inhibitions, make her lose control so humiliatingly? She'd resisted Philip for so long...

But of course that was why. Nature had a habit of suddenly, when least expected, asserting itself. Mia groaned. She hated that derogatory description, 'sex-starved'. Yet didn't it fit? Yes, up to a point. But she'd always believed that sex and love went hand in hand. That sex was an expression of love. She'd never dreamt of responding so passionately to a man she didn't even like.

Still churning inwardly, throat dry as the Sahara, she was making her way towards the bar when she bumped into William and her father talking to a small group of friends and colleagues.

James Fielding was tall and grizzled, a well-built, handsome man still, despite the greyish pallor left by his heart attack. He gave his daughter a disapproving look, as he so often did, and remarked, 'I was wondering where you'd got to.'

At the same moment William beamed at her and asked, 'Enjoying yourself, m'dear?'

'Yes, thank you,' Mia answered as levelly as possible.

At that instant Rhoda appeared out of the throng with Philip, heartbreakingly handsome, at her heels. He didn't seem to be enjoying himself, but Rhoda's smile was scintillating.

'Hello, Mia. Isn't it a lovely party?'

'Lovely,' Mia agreed dutifully, wondering about that look of strain in Philip's light blue eyes. Knowing him, she was aware that he was keyed-up, holding in check some strong emotion. Had they quarrelled? But, if they had, Rhoda showed no signs of it.

In fact the other woman was going on gaily, 'We have some absolutely marvellous news!'

Philip tensed as if about to protest, then thought better of it.

Though Rhoda spoke to the group in general, Mia was oddly convinced that the 'marvellous news' was meant solely for her. A chill of nameless apprehension feathered down her spine.

Flamboyant in scarlet and gold, the redhead put a small, possessive hand through Philip's arm and smiled up at him. 'We've finally got round to setting the date for our wedding, haven't we, darling? In a little over two months' time I'll be Mrs Measham!'

Her words seemed to echo hollowly inside Mia's throbbing head. Dimly she heard the chorus of exclamations and congratulations.

The other woman shot her a quick look that held unmistakable triumph. A look that said plainly, Hands off! He's mine and I'm keeping him!

Without a shadow of doubt, Rhoda knew how she felt about Philip, and the announcement had been carefully planned to hurt and humiliate her in front of other people.

Bathed in heat, yet icy cold and numb inside, Mia lifted her chin. Not looking at Philip, she said carefully, 'I hope you'll be very happy.' She even managed a smile before, on legs that shook almost uncontrollably, she moved away.

Fighting against the shock which was making her feel faint, she set off for the french windows. She was almost there when the room started to spin sickeningly, and she swayed.

A strong arm went around her, and close to her ear a voice murmured, 'It's all right, I've got you. Just lean against me.'

Unable to do anything but obey, Mia lay against Sander Davison while his free hand cradled her head against his shoulder. To anyone noticing, it must have appeared a romantic little dalliance.

Face bent, he spoke to her softly. 'I could carry you, of course, but that would attract rather a lot of undesirable attention. So we'll just wait here until you feel well enough to make it on your own two feet.'

As soon as Mia made an effort to stand upright, he began to walk her slowly towards the terrace. When they were out in the open air, he steered her to a chair tucked away in a dark corner. A firm hand on the nape of her neck, he pushed her head down to her knees.

After a short while she mumbled, 'I feel better now.'

He helped her to sit up, and queried briskly, 'Will you be all right if I leave you alone for a minute?'

'Yes, thank you.' She sounded as polite as a schoolgirl on her best behaviour.

Sander returned quite quickly with, to her surprise, a cup of hot, sweet tea. Her hand was unsteady and, as she tried to drink it, some slopped into the saucer.

'Do you feel able to go back inside?' he asked, when the cup was empty.

'No,' she denied with soft violence.

'You can't stay out here; you're starting to shiver.'

'I just want to go home.' She raised her head. 'I'd like a taxi.'

'That might not be easy. I should imagine every taxi for miles around has already been booked.'

Mia clenched her teeth, which were threatening to chatter. Now what was she to do? She couldn't go back in there under Rhoda's gloating eyes and act as if nothing had happened.

'How did you get here?' Sander questioned abruptly. 'Did you come with your father?'

'No, the Brents gave me a lift. Dad's staying the night.'

'Then I suggest you do the same. I'll go and ask the housekeeper if there's a spare room. If not, you can have mine.'

'Thank you, but I don't want to stay. I *can't* stay!' Some of the desperation Mia was feeling came through.

'Wait here.' Sander's deep voice held a decisive note. He walked away, moving purposefully, but lightly and easily.

As she waited in the shadows, shaking with shock and misery, Mia became vaguely aware that the party seemed to be hotting up. The music was even louder, the sounds of revelry increasing. People were talking, laughing, enjoying themselves, neither knowing nor caring that the bottom had just dropped out of her small world.

After all Philip had said, why had he changed his mind? What weapons had Rhoda used to keep him?

'Have you a coat?' Sander was back by her side.

Mia shook her head. 'No, it was so warm I didn't bring one.'

'Do you want to say goodnight to anyone?' he asked.

'No.'

'Come on, then.'

'Have you managed to get a taxi for me?'

'You could say that.'

With a steadying hand beneath Mia's elbow, he helped her to her feet. Though she was quite tall for a woman, and wearing high heels, the top of her head barely came up to his chin.

Feeling the tremors running through her, Sander shrugged out of his jacket and put it around her shoulders.

'Thank you.' She clutched at the lapels, holding them together over her chest, needing the warmth and comfort it offered.

At the top of the drive there were several taxis, obviously waiting for people, but Sander led her past them and through the packed parking area to a sleek white Porsche.

'This isn't a taxi,' she objected.

'Do you want to go home or not?' he asked shortly.

'Yes, I do.' She put a hand to her throbbing head. 'But I can't take you away from the party like this. What about your . . . girlfriend?'

'Jacqueline will be fine until I get back.' He held open the car door. 'Now suppose we get started.'

Mia climbed in without another word. She didn't want to be beholden to him, of all people, but it appeared she had no choice.

'You don't live with your father, do you?' he asked as he leaned across to fasten her seat-belt.

She shook her head. 'I've a flat in Girton Terrace, Bayswater. Number thirty-three.'

As they drove through the quiet Kentish lanes on their way back to London, Mia leaned her head against the luxurious upholstery and, inexpressibly weary, closed her eyes.

Eyes still closed, she turned her head away to avoid the intrusive finger tapping her cheek.

'Come on,' a deep voice coaxed, 'wake up! It's nowhere near warm enough to sleep in the car all night.'

Mia's heavy lids opened reluctantly. She was slumped in the passenger-seat and in the light from the street lamps she could see Sander Davison leaning over her.

For a moment or two she stared up at him blankly before her sluggish brain provided the answer to what she was doing there. Struggling to sit up, she found they were parked just outside her house.

'Which is your flat?' he asked as he released her safety-belt.

'The basement.'

He came round to open her door. With his jacket still about her shoulders, she got out. Almost immediately she stumbled, and he steadied her.

'You're more than half asleep,' he remarked, as they skirted the black spiky railings and reached the wrought-iron steps that spiralled down to the basement area. 'I'd better go first.' He took her hand and led her as if she were a child.

At the door she gave an exclamation and pressed distracted fingers to her temples. 'I haven't got a key. It was in my bag, and I don't know what happened to that.'

'It's in my jacket pocket,' he told her calmly. 'You left it in the garden.' As he spoke he felt in the pocket nearest to him and, removing her small bag, handed it to her.

Mia groped inside it, her normally agile fingers refusing to perform their allotted task.

'Let me.' Within seconds he'd located her key and turned it in the lock. He opened the yellow-painted door to the familiar groan of rheumaticky hinges.

'Thank you.' Slipping off his jacket, she passed it to him, then, as if not quite sure what to do next, stood swaying slightly in the doorway.

'Unless you intend to invite me in, I suggest you close and lock your door,' he advised crisply.

'I . . . Thank you, you've been very kind.'

She closed the door, fumbling with the chain and pushing the bolt into place. As she put on the light and drew the curtains across the wide window, she heard his car start up and drive away.

Though the place was termed a flat, it was really just a bed-sit, with a small kitchenette and an even smaller bathroom.

Moving slowly, like a robot running out of power, Mia unfolded and made up the bed-settee. Then she undressed, pulled on her nightie, used the bathroom, and crept beneath the duvet. As soon as her head touched the pillow she slept as if pole-axed.

* * *

Floating to the surface, drifting half asleep and half
awake, Mia lay listening to the familiar Sunday
morning sounds of the terrace coming to life: Mrs
Padstow's Rex barking, Miss Ackroyd calling her
Tommy after his night on the tiles, young Trevor
revving his motorcycle...

Then remembrance came, sharp and bitter, bringing
a depression that enshrouded her spirit like a grey
mist. So there it was, the end of all her hopes and
dreams. Better if she'd had neither...

A sudden peal at the doorbell made her heart start
to pound and brought her upright in a single swift
movement. Sitting motionless, hands clenched tightly
together, she fought down the sickening surge of
excitement.

It wouldn't be Philip, she told herself. He wouldn't
come. Sensitive, easily upset, he hated any form of
unpleasantness. Even an argument distressed him. He
wasn't the sort of man to rake over the dead ashes of
a love-affair. If you could call what had been between
them a love-affair...

The bell rang again.

She just couldn't face anyone. She would ignore it.

But the person outside clearly had no intention of
being ignored. Whoever was there had pushed the bell
and kept it depressed with a determination that was
maddening.

Mia struggled out of bed and, unable to locate her
dressing-gown, headed for the door in her loose, daisy-
patterned pink and white cotton nightie.

She felt oddly shaky, lacking in strength, as if she'd
suffered a long, debilitating illness. It was strange how
shock affected both the mind and body.

The bell was still ringing. This early in the morning,
she realised belatedly, it would almost certainly be

young Trevor, wanting some ten-pence pieces for the
tenants' payphone recently installed in the hall.

Having unfastened the bolt and chain, she pushed
up the catch of the Yale lock and flung open the door.
But the tall, well-built man leaning indolently against
the door-frame, his thumb on the bellpush, bore no
resemblance to the skinny youth she was expecting to
see. She felt her cheeks grow hot, and what composure she had left drain away like water down a
plughole, as she looked into the hard face and
mocking green eyes of Sander Davison.

CHAPTER TWO

'Oh, it's *you*!' Mia exclaimed in dismay. He was the very last person she wanted to see, and that must have been only too obvious.

Sander smiled sardonically. His teeth were excellent, his mouth firm and well shaped, with a full lower lip. He really was very attractive, she found herself thinking dispassionately. No wonder women flipped over him!

As he loomed closer, she instinctively fell back. Apparently taking that involuntary movement as an invitation, he followed her into the dimness of the living-room.

His sheer height and breadth of shoulder made the quite large basement appear to shrink drastically.

She retreated further, an agitated hand smoothing the tumbled ash-blonde hair back from her flushed cheeks, her sense of panic aggravated by the unmade bed-settee and her *déshabillé*. 'I—I'm afraid I'm not dressed.'

'So I see. But don't worry about it.' Having given the daisy-strewn nightdress, with its shirred yoke and full skirt, an inspection which bordered on the insolent, he made a grimace and added, 'It's a shade too much like a floral bell tent to turn me on.'

Turning him on was the very last thing she wanted to do! She was about to tell him so when somehow she managed to bite back the retort. It would be playing into his hands, she realised. The best thing was to try to appear calm and in control, and not let him see how easily he could throw her.

She walked to the window, and, drawing aside the curtains, began coolly, 'As it's still quite early and——'

'It's after ten,' he pointed out succinctly, and, apparently quite at ease, lounged back against the tiled fireplace, his elbow on the mantel.

He was casually dressed in light trousers, which moulded his flat stomach and narrow hips, and a fine black turtleneck sweater. His skin was clear and healthy, his green eyes sparkled, and his thick glossy hair curled a little into his neck. He looked fit and sexy and coolly elegant.

Mia took a deep breath and tried again. 'As I wasn't expecting you——'

He struck with the speed of a cobra. 'Who were you expecting? Measham coming hotfoot to assure you that his being married needn't make any difference? That you'd still be able to play your rotten little game on the side?'

Every vestige of colour draining out of her face, she stammered, 'I—I don't know what you mean.'

'Don't try and act the sweet innocent with me— you're wasting your time. I know damn well you two are having an affair!' As she began to shake her head, he said coldly, 'It's no use denying it. Last night, after the party broke up, Rhoda told me what's been going on. It was fortunate she found out in time. You'd almost succeeded in pressurising Measham into breaking his engagement, hadn't you...? *Well, hadn't you?*'

Colour poured back, making Mia's face glow red as a poppy. 'I've never put *any* pressure on Philip! And just supposing I had, how can it possibly be your business?'

He stood facing her, legs slightly apart, hands resting on his lean hips. 'I'm making it my business. For one thing, I'm Rhoda's cousin. We're family. She wants Measham—God knows why, he's a weak, spineless apology for a man. But he's her choice, and I won't stand idly by and see him snatched from under her nose by some immoral little piece with a lovely face and a penchant for other women's men.'

Practically speechless with sheer anger, Mia stuttered, 'Ph-Philip isn't weak and spineless. He's caring and sensitive, not an overbearing, arrogant brute like you... And how dare you call me immoral? You know nothing about me.'

'I know how you behaved last night. If I hadn't been made aware of what kind of woman you are, the way you responded to me then would have given me a pretty good idea.'

'No,' she denied, 'I'm not like that at all. I've never...' She stopped short, unable to admit that *he* was the only man who had ever made her lose control. It would be too humiliating. And even if she *did* admit it, after listening to Rhoda, he wasn't likely to believe *her*.

'You've never...? Do go on with your explanation,' her tormentor urged. 'It sounds most intriguing.'

Taking a deep breath, she said levelly, 'Last night my mind was on Philip, and when I heard your footsteps, for a minute I...I...'

'Thought *I* was *him*... I see.' Sander's tone was acid. 'Well, I'm hardly flattered, but that explains why you threw yourself into my arms with such abandon. What it doesn't explain is why, when you realised I wasn't Measham, you allowed my lovemaking to go on, even invited it.'

Mia shook her head, miserably aware that she had no answer to that. It was so out of character that, even to herself, she couldn't begin to rationalise the way she had acted.

His brilliant eyes on her face, Sander went on remorselessly, 'Either you are the kind of woman I accused you of being, or there's a powerful sexual attraction between us. Which is it?' When she refused to answer, he suggested, 'Both, perhaps? I know——'

'Neither,' she broke in heatedly. 'I've told you, you don't know a thing about me.'

He grinned wolfishly. 'Oh, but I do. Right from our first meeting I knew there was already a man in your life.'

'*How* did you know that?' she asked sharply.

Sander's firm lips took on a rueful twist. 'By your reaction to me. You *were* attracted, but you backed off because you didn't *want* to be. Plainly you had other fish to fry. It didn't occur to me that it was Measham you'd netted.'

'And I suppose it didn't occur to you that, far from being attracted, I backed off, as you put it, because I found you hard and domineering and downright obnoxious?' she demanded furiously. 'Philip's gentle and considerate; he's a fine man who's worth two of you.'

'He's insipid,' Sander said contemptuously. 'A cold fish with no red blood in his veins. Not the man for you, even if he was free. Which he isn't. For better or worse he's Rhoda's future husband, and I can't allow you to come between them.'

Once more rage choked her. '*You* can't allow...!'

'That's right,' Sander agreed calmly. 'Measham's easily led, so make sure you stay away from him.'

As soon as Mia could hold back her anger she said with an attempt at flippancy, 'Working for him as I do, I'm afraid I won't find that too easy.'

The cold gaze pinned her. 'You know quite well what I mean. And don't be too clever, or you won't be working for him much longer.'

'That sounds remarkably like a threat.' Her voice shook, despite all her efforts to keep it steady.

'Let's just say William will do anything for his daughter.'

Mia lifted her chin haughtily. 'In case you've forgotten, my father owns half the firm.'

'Oh, I haven't forgotten. But I very much doubt that James would approve of what's been going on.'

The quiet words struck home like a fist in the solar plexus. How right he was!

'However,' Sander went on smoothly, 'for Measham's sake, Rhoda would prefer no one to know.'

'Then why did she tell you?'

'So I can deal with things.'

A slight smile on her lips, Mia looked him in the face and said scornfully, 'Well, I must say the job of Rhoda's hit-man suits you.'

It took every last ounce of courage not to flinch away from the flashing fury in those green eyes, but somehow she stood her ground.

Almost at once he regained control. His voice level, he said, 'You'll find it won't pay to make cracks like that. Believe me, there's no way you can win, so do as you're told. Leave Measham alone.'

Quivering with indignation, Mia cried, 'And suppose I choose not to, what will you do about it? Have me shot at dawn?'

Sander's white teeth gleamed in a mirthless smile. 'There is an easier, less painful solution.'

'I can't wait to hear it!'

'I can make sure you're too busy keeping my bed warm to even want to stray into his.'

His words made a shiver run through her and her throat went dry. Trying desperately not to let him see how much he affected her, she put on her most disdainful look. 'You only talk about *sex*.' She said it as if it was a dirty word. 'You seem to think that's all there is between Philip and me——'

'*Was,*' Sander corrected pointedly.

Ignoring the interruption, she ploughed on, 'But I *love* him . . .' her beautiful grey eyes filled with tears '. . . and he loves me.'

'You *may* love him, though I beg leave to doubt it, but, if he loves you, why is he marrying another woman in a couple of months' time?'

That was the question Mia had been asking herself. 'I . . . I . . .' To her chagrin the tears overflowed and began to run down her cheeks. She dashed them away with the back of her hand, unwilling to let him see her cry.

His dark, rugged face showing no trace of softening, he went on, 'I understand now why you nearly fainted last night. Rhoda's news came as a shock to you, didn't it? You finally realised you'd lost. No wonder you couldn't wait to get away!'

Mia raised her head, and, with what dignity she could muster, announced, 'If you've said all you have to say, I'd be pleased if you'd go now.'

'I'll go as soon as you give me your word you'll leave Measham alone.'

'What's the matter?' she queried in dulcet tones. 'Is Rhoda afraid I might get him to change his mind again?'

Sander's lips tightened. 'Just give me your word.'

Though she had absolutely no intention of trying to wrest Philip away from Rhoda, Mia was determined not to be browbeaten. Spiritedly she said, 'I won't give any such promise. And, even if I did, you couldn't be sure I'd keep it.'

'I could *make* sure.' His voice held a quiet threat that tightened a silken noose around her throat.

She swallowed hard, refusing to show her fear. 'Oh? And how could you do that?'

'By taking you for my wife.'

Mia's temper reached flashpoint. 'You really are a presumptuous, overweening ... I wouldn't marry you if——'

Holding up a restraining hand, he drawled, 'Please don't say, if I were the last man on earth. You don't mean it.'

'I certainly *do* mean it.'

He shook his head. 'Sex is a powerful incentive, especially to a woman with a nature as ardent as yours.'

From being a small child Mia had done her best to hide her feelings. She'd learnt early how to conceal her sensitivity and warmth, her passionate nature, and consequent vulnerability, beneath a veneer of cool composure.

She'd revealed part of her true character to Philip, but Sander was the only man who had been able to completely strip away that self-possession and see her as she really was.

Disconcerted by his words and the insight they showed, she rushed to deny the charge. 'I'm not——'

'Oh, but you are. That's why we would be right together, and why you and Measham are all wrong for each other. Don't you find him exceedingly tame as a lover? My guess is, you have to hold back in case you scare him half to death.' The green eyes glinted. 'But you didn't hold back with me last night.'

Mia's hands balled into fists. She felt shamed, degraded, unable to bear any more. Brushing past him, she marched to the door and flung it open. 'All right, you've had your say. You've insulted both Philip and me in every possible way. Now get out!'

With a slight shrug of those powerful shoulders, he walked towards her. She couldn't wait to close the door. With him on the *outside*.

Taking her by surprise, he reached a long arm over her shoulder, and before she knew what was happening the door was closed. With him still on the *inside*.

Confounded, she turned with her back to the panels.

A hand each side of her head, he leaned closer, his mouth only an inch or so away, his breath, warm and intoxicating, mingling with hers. 'Perhaps I should refresh your memory?'

Recalling only too well their encounter in the garden, she felt her entire body suffuse with heat. 'No! Leave me alone,' she protested huskily. 'I don't want you to kiss me.'

'Liar,' he said coolly. 'Of course you want me to kiss you. In any case, I wasn't about to ask permission.' Running his fingers into the silky mass of ash-blonde hair, he held her head between his hands, his thumbs spread across her cheeks, and bent to touch his lips to hers.

Clenching her teeth, Mia braced herself to withstand an assault. Sander, however, had none of the bruising clumsiness of some big men. Though masterful, his mouth moved lightly against hers, with a sensuous sweetness that was almost irresistible.

When, with a superhuman effort, she kept her lips tightly closed, his wandered away. They brushed across her temples, her closed eyelids, down her small, neat nose, and followed the clean curve of her jaw to the warm hollow behind her ear, before returning to linger tantalisingly at the corner of her mouth.

Excitement fizzed inside her, rising like the bubbles in champagne. Her lips parted on a gasp and she was lost, all hope of resistance at an end.

He kissed her deeply, passionately, claiming his spoils like the conqueror he was, one hand holding her against him, the other following the curve of her slender buttocks.

She felt the same overwhelming surge of excitement she had experienced the previous night, and was scarcely aware when his hands went to ease the nightdress straps from her shoulders.

Strong, exciting hands, they roamed delicately over her bare back, shaping, stroking, measuring her slim waist, enjoying the satiny smoothness of her skin. Then his fingers, having followed the line of her spine upwards, moved to hold and fondle the soft, naked fullness of her breasts.

Thumbs brushing across her sensitive nipples, teasing and stimulating, started a burning trail of longing that, with the inevitability of a lit fuse travelling towards a keg of dynamite, could end in only one way. Mia made a little whimpering sound deep in her throat, and pressed herself against him.

Sander's laugh was soft, husky, a mixture of pleasure, and triumph. 'See what I mean? What potent chemistry there is between us?' His lips tickling her ear, he added softly, 'It might be a good idea to close the curtains before we move to the bed. We don't want to startle the passers-by, and I plan to make love to you for hours.'

The whispered words sent a shock-wave through her that doused her excitement as quickly and completely as switching off a power source. She stiffened, and made an attempt to push him away.

As if reading her abrupt change of feelings with one hundred per cent accuracy, he let her go and stepped back.

Her hands shook as she pulled the nightdress up to cover herself, but though she was fearful her voice was commendably steady. 'You know what Burns said about the best laid plans of mice and men?'

'Schemes,' Sander corrected her calmly.

Relief running through her like a warm tide, Mia marvelled at his self-control. Knowing that he'd been fully aroused, she'd half expected to have to cope with fury and frustration, possibly even an attempt to force her. But however strong his feelings were, he clearly had them on a tight rein.

Studying her with those clear dark green eyes, he remarked, 'You were co-operating fully, showing as much ardour as any would-be lover could hope for, when whoosh, the fire-nymph was gone, and in her place a snow-queen who could turn any mortal man to ice...What put you off? Was it thoughts of Measham?'

She faced him, tall and slender, her silky ash-blonde hair dishevelled, her cheeks hectically flushed. 'No, it wasn't.' She was shaken to realise it was the truth. Then, with a desire to get back at him, she added sweetly, 'Could it be that you're mistaken and the chemistry *isn't* there?'

'It's there all right.' He regarded her thoughtfully. 'But there's some factor I haven't taken into account, something that doesn't quite fit.'

Mia was wryly amused. What didn't fit was that, far from being easy and experienced, as he obviously thought, for a woman who would be twenty-six on her next birthday she was almost incredibly innocent.

Walking to the door, Sander opened it and turned to say, 'I can't believe you've any *scruples* about sleeping with me before we're married, so if frustration makes you change your mind all you have to do is let me know.' He gave her an ironic little salute, and closed the door behind him.

As she listened to his footsteps ring on the iron stairway, Mia's first sensation was one of relief that he'd finally gone.

Following close on the heels of relief, anger came surging back. How *dared* he come here and tell her what to do? Bully and threaten and revile her! Then try to make love to her! It was too much to bear on top of everything else.

She hated Sander Davison, she thought wildly, *hated* him. And she was disgusted with herself for being so weak. How *could* she have succumbed to his lovemaking a second time? She felt sick and empty, and shook now with nervous reaction.

Sinking down on the edge of the bed, she put a hand to her throbbing head as, over and over again, like a video that wouldn't switch off, memory replayed snatches of the scene that had just taken place.

Stop it, *stop it*! she admonished herself. Making a great effort, she tried to dispel the images. She mustn't keep thinking about it, she must put Sander Davison right out of her mind.

After a while her heart-rate slowed somewhat and she grew fractionally calmer. But, as though imprinted on her retinas, his lean, ruthless face with its strong nose and jaw swam before her, refusing to be banished, and his cool voice saying, 'Before we're married . . .' kept echoing through her head.

Common sense told her that he couldn't *mean* to marry her. But somehow, incredible as it seemed, she knew he did. He was insane! She didn't even like him, much less love him. Philip was the only man she'd ever cared for. She might be *attracted* to Sander Davison, but——

Her train of thought jolted to a halt as if it had run into unseen buffers. She *was* attracted to him . . . At last she admitted what her subconscious had known all along. It was the strength of that attraction, as much as the man himself, which had scared her half to death.

But it was a purely physical thing, she assured herself. There was no way she would marry him. In spite of her protestations, a strange kind of excitement sent shivers running through her. He'd not only talked about a marriage between them as if it was possible, he'd made it sound almost inevitable.

Next morning Mia was up before seven. Thinking of Philip, she felt a cruel ache of emptiness, an agitation of mind and spirit which she was unable to banish.

Showered and dressed, she gulped her coffee, eager to leave the confines of the flat. Sunday had seemed to last for an eternity, and, though worn out by the time she went to bed, she had been quite unable to sleep.

Cold and grey and wet, the first day of April dismally echoed Mia's own mood as she skirted the sagging windowbox, with its few leggy daffodils, and climbed the spiral steps to pavement level.

The Bayswater terrace of once handsome Regency houses was shabby now, doors and window-frames in need of a lick of paint, the cream stucco flaking off in patches, like some unpleasant skin disease.

But, despite the obvious signs of a growing neglect, the rented flats and bed-sits, being central, were at a premium, and Mia—who hated tube travel—considered herself extremely fortunate to have one within walking distance of her place of work.

A blustery wind sprang up, hurling rain beneath her umbrella as, small heels clicking on the wet paving stones with metronome precision, she hurried to reach the glass and concrete fish-tank which housed Rayfield's offices.

'Morning, Miss Fielding. You're early.' The blue-uniformed commissionaire held open the heavy smoked-glass door and gave Mia a smart salute.

She shook the drops from her umbrella and furled it. 'Morning, George. Lumbago any better?'

The burly, middle-aged doorkeeper returned her smile. 'Can't grumble, miss, can't grumble. Though this weather doesn't help.'

In the unaccustomed quiet she crossed the wide lobby and took the lift up to the fourth floor. Stepping out into a deserted foyer, she unlocked the door to the sales director's large, modern office. The inner sanctum was Philip's, the outer area Mia shared with Janet Renshaw, her secretary and right-hand woman.

Mia had just taken off her mac and put her umbrella in the tall ceramic jar which served as a stand when Philip walked in.

Tall and slimly built, wearing a stylish pinstriped business suit, he looked every inch the rising young executive. Carried up in the lift straight from the underground car park, he was bone-dry and immaculate, not a hair out of place.

Her throat choked by a tight knot of tension, Mia just stared at him mutely.

'I hoped you'd be early,' he said, his expression urgent. 'I've got to talk to you. Lord, what a mess! What in heaven's name are we going to do?'

Still unable to utter a word, she shook her head.

Vehemently he declared, 'I can't let you go. I can't!'

Somehow she found her voice. 'It was you who changed your mind.' She bit her lip, knowing she'd sounded reproachful. But mingled with the feeling he always aroused in her was a growing resentment that he'd let her walk blindly into Rhoda's ambush.

He ran an agitated hand over his freshly shaved jaw, and she noticed that his narrow, clean-cut face appeared drawn and tired.

'I'm sorry,' she whispered after a moment, her voice thick with unshed tears. 'But I just don't understand why you *did*, after what you said.'

'I had no choice,' he muttered.

'No choice?'

He tried to meet her eyes and failed, his own sliding away, before he blurted out, 'Rhoda's pregnant.'

'Pregnant?' For a moment Mia failed to understand, then she stared at him aghast. 'You've been sleeping together!'

A flush suffused his fair face. 'You sound like a maiden aunt,' he accused petulantly. 'With engaged couples it's pretty well the norm these days.'

Anger tightened a steel band around Mia's forehead. 'Do you mean to say you were sleeping with her all the time you were trying to talk me into bed ...?'

Philip moved uncomfortably and thrusting his hands into his trouser pockets, jingled some change. 'You know very well it's *you* I love. But by the time I realised that, Rhoda and I were already... I mean...it was too late. If I'd suddenly cooled off she'd have wondered why...'

Brushing his words aside, Mia demanded furiously, 'What would you have done if I'd agreed? Allotted us alternate nights?'

'There's no need to make me out to be some kind of callous monster,' he protested. Pulling his hands from his pockets, he spread them, palms uppermost, in a gesture of supplication. 'If only Rhoda hadn't got pregnant everything would have been all right.'

'You mean you could have gone ahead and broken your engagement, and I'd have been none the wiser?'

'That's not a very nice thing to say!' Philip both looked and sounded wounded.

'It's not a very nice thing to do!' Her smoky-grey eyes held contempt.

He ran restless fingers through his blond, expertly styled hair. 'You *wanted* me to break things off, didn't you?'

'Yes,' she admitted. 'But then I had no idea you were...' she choked on the word '...lovers.'

'I can't see what difference that makes.'

Dear God, how insensitive could he be?

'Please, darling, listen,' he begged. 'There's no reason for you to be jealous. It's *you* I really love and want. And at least, working in the same office, we can *see* each other every day until I can figure out some way for us to be together.'

Mia swallowed past the painful lump in her throat. 'It's far too late for that. And we won't be working in the same office. For everyone's sake, I'm giving in my notice.'

Seizing her hand, he gripped it almost painfully. 'Now you're just being silly. There's absolutely no need for you to leave. It's not as if——'

'I couldn't bear to stay,' she interrupted. 'And even if I could, now Rhoda's pregnant it's not fair to cause her any more worry.'

Philip's smooth head came up. 'What do you mean, any more worry? She doesn't know there's ever been anything between us.'

'Of course she knows!'

'I didn't say anything to her. I'd planned to leave it until after the party. Then as soon as I got there, she told me . . . her news. So what makes you think she knows?'

'I don't *think*, I'm certain of it.'

'How *could* she know?' Philip looked horrified.

'I haven't the faintest idea how she found out, but——'

The office door opened and Janet walked in.

Guiltily, Philip dropped Mia's hand, and, turning on his heel, disappeared into his own office without returning the secretary's 'Good morning.'

Not seeming to notice, she was struggling with a knot pulled in the fastening of her rain-hood, while she muttered uncomplimentary things about the British climate.

Janet was in her late twenties, small and vivacious, with short black hair and beautiful liquid brown eyes in a pointed gamine face.

Without being confidantes, the two women had always got on well together, and were good friends.

'Isn't it foul?' she said, as the hood finally came free and she hung both that and her mac on the coatstand. 'Whoever it was wrote, "Oh, to be in England, now that April's there . . ." took jolly good care to be somewhere more clement!'

'Robert Browning,' Mia said, trying to sound as if nothing was amiss. 'His "Home-Thoughts, From Abroad".'

Janet patted her dark bob into place and sighed deeply. 'Abroad—now there's an appealing thought. Greece, for instance, or southern Italy . . . Somewhere the sun is shining.'

'We've just had several lovely sunny days,' Mia pointed out.

The dark girl grunted. 'I find it only whets my appetite for more. Ah, well . . . to work. What joys have we lined up for today?' After a quick glance through the contents of the in-tray, she added, 'Plenty, it seems. Will you be dealing with——?'

'I have to go out,' Mia said quickly. 'I'm afraid you'll have to cope as best you can.'

With the equability that had made her invaluable, Janet only asked, 'If you're not back before lunch, do you want me to send out for a sandwich and hold the fort?'

'Yes, please, if you wouldn't mind.'

On leaving the building, Mia found it was raining even harder, and the squally wind had strengthened, making conditions diabolical.

Cold and desolate, spirits at zero, she tilted her brown umbrella, adorned with orange sunflowers, to keep the worst at bay, and hurried along the streaming pavement towards the nearest job agency.

There was nothing for it but to leave Rayfield's. If she asked for a move to another department, both her father and William would want to know why. And there was no way she could stay working for Philip.

She'd loved and believed in him for so long, put him on a pedestal. Finding him capable of such perfidy had cut the emotional ties as sharply as a guillotine, and, like a guillotine, had left her bleeding.

Never once had it occurred to her that he might be deceiving *both* of them, sharing Rhoda's bed while he tried to persuade *her* to sleep with him. How could he? she wondered bitterly.

And to cap it all he was still insisting he didn't want to give her up. So what did he want? Rhoda as his wife and her as his mistress, as Sander Davison had suggested?

Some two and a half hours later she left the third agency more depressed than ever, if that were possible. They had taken down her particulars and she was 'on the books' of all three. But none of them had been able to offer her the kind of job she wanted, at the salary she *needed* to keep her flat.

She felt as if a sudden hurricane had blown apart the whole fabric of her life, leaving her stumbling amid the ruins. It seemed that soon she might have nothing left, no Philip, no job, no place even to live.

She couldn't bring herself to go back to her father's large, gloomy house. In any case, he wouldn't *want* her back. He'd been relieved when, after leaving the secretarial college, she'd opted for independence.

A van going past at speed sprayed her legs with muddy water and she shivered in the arctic wind, her slim ankles numb, her feet like ice.

While she waited, with a bedraggled little group of pedestrians, to cross Oxford Street, a treacherous gust nearly succeeded in snatching the umbrella from her hand.

As she fought to control it, the thin heel of her right court shoe slipped into a crack between the pavement and the kerb and was held fast.

Before she could make any attempt to free it, the lights changed and people began to barge past, irritated by the hold-up. 'Damn!' she muttered, tugging uselessly, hampered by the brolly.

'Take your foot out,' a deep, only too familiar voice instructed.

CHAPTER THREE

MIA swung round, her heart racing, the sunflower brolly waving about wildly.

A hand closed around her wrist, taking control, and the mocking voice added, 'You're really not safe with that thing.'

'You again!' she said accusingly.

'Full marks,' Sander Davison accorded with exaggerated patience. 'Now, not only are we getting wet through, but my car's causing a traffic jam, so be a good girl and take your foot out.'

Seeing no alternative, she obeyed him, standing stork-like on one leg while he crouched to ease the trapped heel free.

'There!' He gave a grunt of satisfaction and slid the court shoe back on to her foot. Then, towering over her once more, he removed the umbrella from her grasp, and having closed it, put a hand beneath her elbow and hurried her to where his car was holding up the flow of vehicles. Opening the front passenger door, he instructed briefly, 'Get in.'

'I don't want to get in.' Mia pulled back, her face mulish. 'I don't want anything——'

'Do as I say, and don't argue.' He fairly bundled her into the Porsche and slammed the door. 'Fasten your seat-belt,' he ordered as he slid in beside her.

Muttering a rebellious, 'Bossy devil,' she did as she was bidden.

Sander clicked his tongue reprovingly. 'Now is that any way to speak to your rescuer? You should be thanking me nicely.'

Scowling, she said a short, 'Thank you.'

'How gracious!' he purred.

Becoming aware that she was behaving badly, she felt her cheeks grow warm.

Looking straight ahead, he smiled a little, as if satisfied that he'd made her feel in the wrong.

'Where are you taking me?' she asked sharply, as, driving down New Bond Street, they headed for Mayfair.

He gave her a lascivious grin. 'Where do you think? To my cave, of course, where I propose to strip you naked and ravish you to my heart's delight...and yours,' he added softly.

The rider, and the erotic images his words evoked, sent even more colour flooding into her face, and made her entire skin prickle with moisture. Knowing it was what he had hoped for, she bit her lip in vexation.

Chilled and dreary, feeling at her lowest ebb, the last thing she wanted was to have to cope with Sander Davison. But it seemed she had no choice. He was so vigorous and vital that trying to oppose him was like trying to blow against the wind.

In just a few minutes they were drawing up outside a large Georgian house in Crombie Square. An arm around her waist, Sander hurried Mia through the pouring rain and up a short flight of stone steps to a porticoed entrance.

As they walked into a nicely furnished hall with a broad, elegant sweep of staircase, an elderly woman wearing a neat blue dress emerged from a door at the far end.

'Ah, Mrs Rose,' Sander said, 'can you rustle up a spot of lunch for Miss Fielding and myself?'

'Certainly, sir,' she replied civilly, and bustled off.

A hand cupping Mia's elbow, Sander escorted her into a high, well-proportioned room with an Adam fireplace and long windows which looked out over the quiet square. Though luxurious in every respect, it was lived-in and comfortable, with framed snapshots, lots of books, a glowing fire, and bowls of tulips and daffodils.

Mia, who was very sensitive to atmosphere, immediately felt at home. Or would have done if it hadn't been for the disturbing presence of her host.

'Let me help you off with your things.'

A glint in his eye warred with the guileless words and made her quiver. Trying not to let it show, she unfastened the belt and buttons and allowed him to slip her mac and rayon scarf from her shoulders.

As he did so, he picked up a handful of her hair and ran it through his fingers as if it fascinated him. It wasn't the fine, fly-away hair of some natural blondes, but a heavy, silky mass that, having no great appreciation of her own looks, Mia considered her main asset.

'Come and sit by the fire,' he suggested, throwing on a couple of logs and stirring them into a blaze with the toe of a handmade shoe.

When she sat down on the low couch, he stooped, and, pulling off her shoes, turned them on to their sides to dry. She was thrown into even greater confusion when he took first one, then the other of her slender feet between his palms and began to chafe some life back into them.

The oddly intimate gesture made her all at once feel cared for, cherished. But of course that was nonsense. Sander Davison had no tender feelings towards her. Just the opposite, in fact.

As he straightened and took a seat beside her she hitched over on the soft cushions, putting as much space as possible between them.

'Do you need to move away?' he asked.

'Do you need to sit so close?' she retorted.

'Why?' His eyes gleamed with amusement. 'Do I disturb you?'

The short answer to that was yes, she felt positively *threatened*, but she chose to ignore the provocative question and, spreading her palms to the flames, remarked, 'I understand you've been living in Hong Kong?'

'Yes, I was out there for almost five years handling the bank's Far East transactions.'

'Will you be going back?' she asked hopefully.

He shook his head, with an ironic smile. 'Sorry. I'm home for good.'

'Do you live here alone?' It was a thoughtless question and she regretted it instantly.

A glint in his eye, he answered, 'I do at the moment.'

Hurriedly she went on, 'I mean, it seems a big house for only one.'

'Far too big,' he agreed. 'But it used to be our family home, so I've a certain fondness for it.'

'You've no family left?'

'No, my father died recently; that's why I came home... My mother was killed in a plane crash six years ago.

'William was very cut up about it. Though they'd seen very little of one another after they were grown up, she'd always been his favourite sister.

'My father never really got over her death. He immersed himself in his work, and virtually lived at the bank rather than come home to a big empty house.'

Stretching his long legs indolently, his eyes on Mia's face, Sander added, 'After we're married we can sell it and buy something smaller, easier to manage.'

Determinedly ignoring both his reference to their marriage and his gaze, she stared into the fire and visualised the kind of rustic cottage she'd always dreamed of having.

'Perhaps you'd like to live in the country?'

Mia gave him a quick, startled look. The way he at times knew exactly what she was thinking was disconcerting to say the least, but still she said nothing.

'How soon are you planning to leave Rayfield's?' Smoothly he changed tack.

'How do you know I'm planning to leave?'

'I caught sight of you coming out of the job agency.' He slanted her a glance. 'I found it difficult to make up my mind which way a woman like you would jump.'

Frostily she repeated what she'd said to him once before, 'You don't know what kind of woman I am. You don't really know me at all.'

'But I intend to.' He moved suddenly, taking her head between his long, well-shaped hands. His thumbs stroking hypnotically over her cheekbones, his voice a husky murmur, he went on, 'I intend to know you mind and body, every single thing about you. What makes you laugh, what makes you cry, how you think, how you feel, how you look when you're asleep, what you sound like when I make love to you...'

She was wide-eyed, mesmerised, waiting for that hovering mouth to close over hers. When it did she made a little sound almost like a moan, her heavy lids shut and she began to tremble.

There was a tap at the door and the housekeeper came in. 'Soup, sandwiches, and coffee,' she said. 'I hope that will be all right?'

'Fine, thank you, Mrs Rose.' Sander sounded as cool and unruffled as if they'd been sitting discussing the weather.

Mia, who had jerked free, hurriedly bent her head to hide the surge of embarrassed colour. To her relief the woman put the tray down on the coffee-table and departed without so much as a glance.

Picking up the jug, Sander poured soup into two bowls, remarking mockingly, 'There's no need to look so ruffled. Mrs Rose is always very discreet.'

'I should imagine she needs to be,' Mia opined scathingly. Avoiding looking at him, she unfolded a snowy napkin, rested the bowl on her knees, and began to spoon up the soup. It was a delicious minestrone, thick and satisfying.

For a while they ate in silence, then, his tone tinged with derision, he remarked, 'Leaving Rayfield's is quite a clever move. Your own idea? Or does Measham think it will be easier to carry on your affair if you appear to have severed all connection?'

Clenching her teeth in futile anger, Mia resisted the blatant attempt to provoke her into fighting back.

When she failed to rise to the bait, Sander went on, 'Why didn't you tell him it was all over, that you were going to be my wife?'

She took a deep, steadying breath. 'You can't be serious about tying yourself to a woman you obviously despise, just for your cousin's sake!'

'It isn't solely for Rhoda's sake. I need a wife.'

He offered Mia a sandwich before continuing, 'The Davison Lazenby Merchant Bank was founded in the early 1900s by my grandfather. The old man was a diehard; so was my father. He had an almost Victorian

attitude towards home and family, and strongly dis-
approved of what he regarded as the lax ethics of today's generation.

'Before I can take my father's place as head of the
bank, under the terms of his will I have to be respectably married.'

Cynically he went on, 'There are plenty of beautiful women about, but, as far as I'm concerned, a
lovely face is no compensation for an empty head.
Though your morals leave quite a lot to be desired,
you have the combination of brains and beauty I've
been looking for. Treated with a firm hand, you
should fit the bill nicely...'

Apart from that stinging reference to her morals,
Mia might almost have been flattered if he hadn't
added that last autocratic sentence.

Swallowing the last mouthful of her chicken
sandwich, she controlled her anger with an almost
visible effort, and tried to use sweet reason. 'If beauty
is a prerequisite, then I don't "fit the bill", as you
put it.'

Unmoved, he answered, 'I'll be the judge of that.'

She made another attempt. 'But you can't marry
so cold-bloodedly!'

His voice full of meaning, Sander assured her,
'That's the last thing it's likely to be. I'm sure our
husband-and-wife relationship will generate a fair
amount of heat.'

She shook her head. 'I won't be your wife.'

'You haven't much choice.'

Boldly she threw down the gauntlet. 'Of course I
have a choice. You can't *make* me marry you.'

'I wouldn't take any bets on that.'

He was so sure of himself that the short hairs on
the back of her neck rose. 'W-what do you mean?'

'I'm leaving for Amsterdam tonight, but before I catch the flight I'm having a meeting with your father. A private financial discussion.'

Stormy grey eyes on his face, Mia waited, knowing there had to be more.

'Do you remember when Yanus Pharmaceuticals was up for grabs? William didn't think it was safe and refused to touch it, but James borrowed heavily from the bank and bought a large block of shares. The crash was sudden when it came. Overnight his shares became worthless bits of paper.'

Though she hadn't known of her father's involvement, Mia recalled the crash. It was about that time James had suffered his heart attack.

Pulling herself together, she asked slowly, 'You mean my father owes you a great deal of money?'

'I mean I could ruin him.'

Her eyes darkened to charcoal. 'That's blackmail!'

He lifted wide shoulders in a slight shrug. 'Let's call it friendly persuasion. I made a promise to Rhoda and I intend to keep it, whatever means I need to use.'

Feverishly Mia sought for a way to escape. 'Look, what if I leave Rayfield's at once and don't go back?'

'I intend you to do that anyway.' His voice was tempered steel.

'If I promise never to see Philip again . . .?'

'As you yourself pointed out, I can't be sure you'd keep your word. And you're forgetting that I need a wife.'

Endeavouring to stay calm, Mia once more stared at the blazing logs, presenting him with a pure profile—a small, straight nose, the curl of long lashes, the curve of a high cheekbone, a softly rounded chin. 'But what about your girlfriend?' she asked, adding drily, 'Surely she has the qualifications you mentioned?'

'Not really. I want a wife I can talk to, who can share my life as well as my bed. Jacqueline is intelligent enough, but too single-minded, too taken up with herself and her own career to make anyone a good wife.'

'So you want me for a wife and her for a mistress?' Mia asked scornfully.

Sander shook his head. 'One willing woman is enough.'

'But I'm not willing.'

'Aren't you?' he asked softly, suggestively.

Feeling warmth that had nothing to do with the fire stealing into her cheeks, Mia said quickly, 'Surely there must be plenty of eligible women who'd be only too pleased to marry you.'

'I don't want "plenty of women"—I want you.' A hand took her chin, turning her face towards him, and those eyes, dark and clear, with tiny pinpoints of gold trapped in their jade depths, looked straight into hers. 'I want you more than I thought it possible to want any woman, and I mean to have you.'

The impact of his words, his look, made her head spin and her whole body flush with heat.

Then, cool as a cucumber, he was sitting back checking his watch. 'Unfortunately I have an appointment at two-thirty. Perhaps you'll pour the coffee?'

Doing her best to appear unruffled, she picked up the delicate black and gold pot. 'How do you like it?'

He grinned wickedly. 'Hot and strong and sweet, the same way I like my loving.'

She wished she hadn't asked.

As soon as they'd both finished their coffee, he put down his cup and told her with a touch of wry humour, 'I'll be in Amsterdam until Friday, so you've a few days free of me.'

When she chose to ignore his teasing, he murmured smoothly, 'Now, where can I take you? Are you heading for home?'

'Can you drop me off at the office?'

He gave her a rapier-like glance.

Though she hadn't intended to, Mia found herself explaining hurriedly, 'I won't be staying, but I have to hand in my notice and clear my desk.'

Just before he turned away she caught the flare of triumph in his handsome, heavy-lashed eyes, and realised belatedly that her hasty words had been taken to mean surrender.

While he went upstairs to fetch his suitcase, Mia pulled on her shoes and took her mac and scarf from where he'd draped them over a chair.

When she was installed in the car, and Sander had put his case in the boot, he slid in beside her and reached across to push home the clip of her seat-belt.

The rain-misted windows seemed to isolate them in their own private little world. His nearness, the pressure of his muscular thigh against her leg, sent shock-waves running along her nerve-ends.

He felt the tremor she couldn't control and asked, 'Warm enough?'

'Quite warm enough, thank you,' she replied, her creamy-complexioned face determinedly schooled into a composed mask, her grey eyes clear and untroubled.

As if hating to see her so apparently serene, his eyes lit with a gleam of devilment and he reached to tuck a shining tendril of hair behind her ear. Mia wanted to move away, but in the confines of the passenger-seat she was unable to. Trapped, she sat as if turned to marble while his index finger slid down to trace her lovely mouth, before touching and lingering on the fluttering pulse at the base of her throat.

His dark face was only inches away, and she breathed in the subtle scent of his aftershave. Staring at his lips, she was hypnotised, unable to look away, her own waiting for their touch.

Voice deep and seductive, he murmured, 'Kiss me—you know you want to.'

Her breath caught in her throat, and she half shook her head, trying to deny that fatal attraction. His mouth hovered, then, light as thistledown, brushed against hers. She was unable to help herself; her lids closed, and her soft lips parted. Drowning in pleasure, she waited for him to deepen the kiss, but almost immediately he drew back, leaving her bereft.

Her eyes opened with a jerk as the engine purred into life and the car swished away. Feeling incredibly foolish, angry with him for tantalising her, even more aggravated with herself for betraying how much he affected her, Mia turned her head to stare resolutely through the rain-spattered window.

For a while the only sound in the car was the swish of busy wiper-blades, then Sander broke the silence to say casually, 'Before I leave for Amsterdam, I'll make all the arrangements for a special licence, so we can be married as soon as I get back.'

Panic stopped her breath and held her rigid while her mind raced. She *couldn't* let herself be blackmailed into being his wife. Yet what alternative had she? Though Sander was going easy on the pressure, it was there, just beneath the surface. If she refused to go through with this marriage, he might well be ruthless enough to ruin her father.

'There's no need to look so distraught,' he said cynically. 'I don't think, wanting me as you do, you'll find sharing my bed too much of a hardship.'

He was right, damn him. She *did* want him, she admitted that now without reservation. Each time she looked at him there was that tiny lick of flame, and the thought of his touching her brought her out in goose-bumps.

Yet how *could* she want him so much when, until that very morning, her whole life had revolved around another man?

It was completely irrational, and she couldn't begin to explain it. She only knew she did. Sander overwhelmed her senses in a manner that made nonsense of her attempts at resistance. Facing the truth, she knew that if she'd loved *him* there was no way she could have held out against him, as she'd held out against Philip.

She tried to look at her feelings for Philip objectively, and for the first time asked herself, had it really been love? She'd wanted, *needed* to love and be loved. But hadn't she fooled herself on both counts? Hadn't what she'd felt for him been a kind of dependence, a hero-worship mingled with gratitude? While his 'love' for her had been a travesty of the word...

With a squelch of tyres the big car drew to a halt in front of the office block. Ignoring the rain wetting his dark hair and soaking into the shoulders of his grey business suit, Sander came round to open her door.

By the time she'd clambered out, he had her umbrella up. 'Make the fond farewell a final one,' he warned, adding with careless confidence, 'And try not to look so fraught! Once we're married I'll soon help you forget Measham.'

Riled by such easy assurance, Mia flashed, 'What makes you think I want to forget him?'

Sander's lips compressed. Curtly he said, 'I'll ring you from Amsterdam,' and, jumping back in the Porsche, drove away.

Standing on the shiny pavement, she stared after the sleek white car, despite everything, feeling a strange regret that they'd parted on such an angry note.

A sudden spiteful gust of wind snatched at the umbrella, almost turning it inside out. Collecting herself, she swung on her heel and hurried into the building.

When she reached the sales office it proved to be empty, and the door to the inner office was closed. Pausing only to pull off her mac, Mia sat down at her desk, rolled a piece of paper into the typewriter, and typed out her resignation. She gave no reason, merely stated that she would be leaving immediately.

She'd only just folded the paper and put it into an envelope when Janet came in clutching a sheaf of pamphlets she'd been photocopying.

'So you're back!' the dark girl exclaimed thankfully. 'Philip's been asking for you. He seemed very put out that you weren't here.'

'Oh . . .' Mia said flatly. 'Is he . . .?'

'He had to go out himself. He'll be gone until about four o'clock this afternoon.'

Mia breathed an audible sigh of relief. She didn't want to have to face Philip again. There was nothing left to say.

Brown eyes curious, Janet remarked, 'You look in a bit of a tizzy. Is something wrong?'

'I'm leaving Rayfield's.'

'Leaving!' The other girl looked thunderstruck. 'How soon?'

'Straight away,' Mia said with determination. 'I'm sorry to dump everything into your lap like this, but I . . .' She hesitated, wondering what explanation she could give for just walking out.

Janet frowned. 'No wonder Philip's looking so upset! Still, it's probably for the best. There's no future in loving a man who isn't free to love you back...' A hot tide of colour running up into her thin face, she stopped speaking abruptly. 'I... I'm sorry,' she stammered. 'I shouldn't have said that. I didn't mean to...' Then, miserably, 'Oh, hell! I'm only making it worse.'

Mia sat motionless, transfixed. After a moment or two she asked with laudable steadiness, 'Was it *so* obvious?'

'No... Well, yes...' Janet gave a heartfelt groan. Taking a grip on herself, she said with care, 'I don't mean obvious to all and sundry. In fact I'm sure no one else knew or even suspected. If they had, there would have been gossip, and how!

'But one day when Philip was standing by your desk I happened to glance up and I noticed the way you were looking at each other. I'm sorry... It was stupid to let my tongue run away with me and upset you even more...'

Seeing the other girl was genuinely worried, Mia said firmly, 'You haven't upset me. What little there was between Philip and me is over. Ended.'

'So do you *have* to go?' Janet asked practically.

'I *want* to.'

'But surely instead of leaving you could get transferred to another department?'

Mia shook her head. 'I'd rather go. It makes it easier for everyone. You see, you weren't the only one to know. Rhoda found out.'

'Oh, lord! I suppose that put the proverbial cat among the pigeons? Is the engagement off?'

Mia shook her head. 'No, she and Philip are getting married in a few weeks' time.'

'Oh, I see.'

Clearly Janet presumed that that was the real reason she was leaving.

'Good jobs aren't easy to come by these days.' The girl sounded concerned. 'Have you got another lined up?'

'No.' Then, without really meaning to, Mia found herself adding, 'But possibly I won't need one. I might be getting married myself.'

'Married!' Janet gaped. 'You did say *getting married*?'

Mia was regretting having said anything, but it was patently too late. 'Yes, I——'

'Well, don't keep me in suspense, tell me who it is you might be marrying.' Janet's brown eyes were bright with excitement and curiosity.

Swallowing, Mia admitted, 'Sander Davison.'

Janet whistled. 'Lucky you! He could have the top off my egg any time.' Then, bubbling over, 'I always thought he fancied you. Whenever he came into the office he never took his eyes off you. But I didn't expect... I mean, it's so sudden. I hadn't even re-alised you knew him that well. So when did things hot up?'

'He was at Rhoda's party on Saturday night, and he took me home.' When it became obvious that Janet was expecting more, Mia added reluctantly, 'Then he called at my flat the next morning.'

The other girl was agog. 'Unless it's a state secret, tell me the rest. When did he actually ask you to marry him?'

Mia wondered briefly what Janet would have to say if she told her the truth, that she hadn't been *asked*, but *blackmailed* into it.

Trying to appear nonchalant, she gave an edited version of the morning's events, ending weakly, 'But I haven't really had time to think.'

'What is there to think about? Unless you're still in love with...? Sorry, forget I asked that.'

'No, I'm not still in love with Philip.' As Mia said it, she knew without a doubt that it was the truth. 'I'm not sure I ever was.'

Janet sighed. 'Well, I'm delighted for you, I really am. From what I know of Sander Davison, he strikes me as being twice the man Ph... There I go again! This seems to be my day for letting my tongue run away with me...

'Anyway, if you find yourself in need of a bridesmaid I'm in practice. If you remember, my sister got married a couple of months back.'

'Yes, I——'

'So how soon do you think it will be?' the girl rushed on eagerly.

'S-Sander...' Mia stumbled a little over the name '...said he was going to arrange for a special licence, so we can be married when he gets back from Amsterdam in a few days' time.'

'Not a man to hang around,' Janet commented approvingly. 'But then I never thought he would be.' She glanced at the clock. 'Talking of hanging around, if I don't get on with some work *I'll* be needing another job!'

While Janet got down to it, Mia went through her desk drawers and removed her few personal belongings. Then, having put her letter of resignation on Philip's desk, she pulled on her mac.

Janet looked up, and, a shade hesitantly, asked, 'Does Philip...? I mean, have you...?'

'I told him I was leaving. I'd sooner he didn't know anything else.'

Whatever Janet's thoughts were she kept them to herself, merely promising, 'The Sphinx has nothing on me.' After a moment she tacked on a shade awkwardly, 'I'll miss you. Now don't forget to keep in touch.'

'I won't,' Mia promised. Feeling unable to face all the questions her leaving so suddenly would be bound to provoke, she slipped away without saying goodbye to anyone.

The wind and rain had abated somewhat, but April was still grizzling like a fretful baby as she made her way home. Usually walking cleared her head and made thinking easier, but not this time. She felt positively punch-drunk, reeling from the effects of so much happening so quickly.

Eventually, her head aching dully, Mia pushed away the confusion of thoughts. She wouldn't try to think any more. She would wait until she wasn't so tired and her brain was clearer before she made any further effort to sort out her feelings and her life.

CHAPTER FOUR

ABOUT half-past nine that evening, Mia was curled up in front of the electric fire, trying vainly to keep her mind on the book she was holding, when there was a knock at the door. She hesitated, suddenly fearful that it might be Philip.

Almost immediately common sense told her it wouldn't be. Apart from disliking any unpleasantness, he must have realised there was no way he could change her mind about leaving. Rhoda would want her gone and, as things were, he couldn't afford to rock the boat.

She opened the door to find Trevor on the step. In close-fitting beige trousers, his bony elbows jutting through a tight, straw-coloured jumper, he put her in mind of a stick insect.

'Phone for you,' he informed her. 'And can you lend me a couple of ten-pence pieces?' A red-haired Lothario, he invariably had more than one eager girl-friend awaiting his call.

Reaching for her purse, Mia fished for the coins.

'Thanks.' He grinned at her. 'You're a doll!'

It was fine now, so, pausing only to check that she had her key, she followed him up the spiral steps and into the main entrance of the house. The phone was at the far end of the bare hallway, its receiver dangling.

She picked it up and said a cautious, 'Hello?'

Sander's deep, attractive voice asked, 'Missed me?' Her heart began to thud, but, taking a stand against such easy self-assurance, she enquired coolly, 'Who is it speaking?'

He laughed, and said appreciatively, 'Cat!' adding briskly, 'Now I've only got a couple of minutes, so be a good girl and listen. I've made all the arrangements for a special licence. We're to be married by the Reverend Peter Jenkins at twelve o'clock this Saturday, at St Giles' Church, Mayfair.'

'You're going much too fast for me,' she protested helplessly. 'I need more time.'

Deliberately misunderstanding her, he said equably, 'Now you're not working, four days should be ample time to do your shopping. Go to Harrods. I've cleared it for you to get everything you need for the wedding and a trousseau put on my account.'

With no idea of what kind of wedding he was envisaging, she stammered, 'B-but what do you want me to get, a suit or a...?' Only when the question was out did she realise her answer had confirmed that, subconsciously at least, she'd made up her mind to go through with it.

'Though in your case it may not be appropriate, for the look of the thing a white wedding-dress, a veil, and all the trimmings.'

She was still smarting from the edge of scorn in his voice when he went on, 'I've talked to your father, and, though he was understandably surprised by the suddenness, he's agreed to give you away... If you want to speak to him yourself, it will have to be to-night. He's leaving first thing in the morning on a business trip and won't be back until late Friday night.

'Now have you a friend who would be your bridesmaid?' he added.

'Janet ... Janet Renshaw.'

'Ah, yes... Then take her with you and get what she needs. Have everything sent to Crombie Square. You'll be leaving from there.'

'But I——'

'One last thing, I take it you have a current passport?'

'Yes, I——'

'Good. Make sure it's handy. And Mia, feel free to lash out on the spending, the bank balance will stand it. Take care of yourself. I'll be in touch.'

Before she could say a word, there was a click and the line went dead.

Feeling as if she'd been run over by a steamroller, Mia stood for a full minute before she depressed the receiver-rest and, dipping in her purse for some change, dialled her father's number.

Their relationship had always been a difficult one, and, though Mia had tried hard, there had never been any *real* communication between them. But surely he would want to talk to her about her wedding?

He didn't, and any fear she'd entertained that he might ask awkward questions was soon set at rest.

'I suppose you know what you're doing?' he demanded irritably. 'A man like Sander Davison, who's always had his pick of beautiful women, can be hard to hold. Rhoda tried and got nowhere.'

'Rhoda?' Mia was startled. 'Do you mean she was in love with him?'

'William told me that a few years back she was mad about the man. Apparently most of the feeling was on her side, and things finally fizzled out when he went off to Hong Kong. Eventually she settled for Measham.'

Having cleared his throat, James went on, 'I can't help but feel that a man as tough as Davison is right out of your league. Still, if he's prepared to marry you...'

It was clear that the suddenness had given her father totally the wrong idea.

Hurt, she wondered briefly what he would say if she told him the truth. But of course she couldn't do that. Instead she said, 'He doesn't *have* to marry me. I'm not pregnant, if that's what you think.'

James gave a grunt, which clearly conveyed that he'd wait and see, and replaced the receiver.

Had Sander indulged in an affair with Rhoda? Mia wondered, as she slowly made her way back to the basement. Was his concern for his cousin, his determination that she shouldn't lose Philip, due to guilt that *he'd* gone off to Hong Kong and left her?

After a disturbed night, Mia slept late next morning and awoke with a strange sense of unreality. She made herself some coffee and, feeling like an actress with a new role in a play, who was still uncertain of her part, phoned Janet to query, 'Will you be able to get away at lunchtime?'

'Yes, if I ask Tessa or one of the others to fill in for me. When and where shall I meet you?'

'Harrods, at twelve-thirty.'

'What's wrong with the local wine-bar?' Janet wanted to know.

'They don't sell bridesmaids' dresses,' Mia told her.

Janet was early, and fairly bursting with excited questions, most of which Mia managed to answer as they made their way to the bridal department.

There, the feeling of unreality persisting, she chose an ivory wedding-gown in wild silk, which fitted her to perfection. It was beautiful and romantic, with full, rustling skirts, and a shoulder-length gossamer veil held by a pearl coronet.

Then it was Janet's turn to select a pretty shell-pink bridesmaid's dress with matching shoes and a headband.

That achieved, the pair made their way to the coffee-bar. As she tucked into her prawn salad and granary bread, Janet said, 'Can I ask you something? I could see Sander was attracted to you from the word go, but you always seemed set on avoiding him. What made you change your mind?'

'It hasn't occurred to you that I might be marrying him for his money?' Mia asked with an attempt at banter.

Janet snorted. 'Do me a favour! I think I know you better than that. But up until a few days ago you seemed to positively dislike him. Or was that just a form of self-defence?'

'You're getting warmer,' Mia told her drily.

'Well, I'm jolly glad things have turned out like this,' the other girl said. 'I didn't like to see you wasting your life on a man who wasn't free.' Spearing her last pink, succulent prawn, she added, 'So what plans have you for the big day?'

Mia repeated what little she'd been told, adding, 'I won't know any more until I've heard from Sander again.'

When a reluctant Janet had hurried back to the office, Mia set about shopping for her trousseau. Aware that if she was going to be Sander's wife she would need to look the part, she chose a whole new wardrobe, spending with a recklessness that shocked her when she thought about it later.

She selected three dresses, several skirts and tops with co-ordinated jackets, and, bearing in mind that Sander had asked about her passport, a very special going-away suit with matching accessories.

In the lingerie department she went quite mad. She'd always adored pretty undies, the brush of silk against her skin, and now, with a feeling of anticipation she preferred not to analyse, she chose a selection of the most beautiful, filmy things on display.

With a kind of reverence, the salesgirl produced a gossamer nightdress and matching négligé, lovely and delicate as a spider's web, and suggested, 'If you're buying a trousseau . . . ?'

Hesitating only briefly over the set's virginal whiteness, Mia said a shade breathlessly, 'I'll take it,' and thought defiantly that though at first Sander might look at it with derision, knowledgeable as he undoubtedly was, he would soon realise he'd been mistaken.

Then a sudden uneasy thought occurred to her. Having expected an experienced woman, a woman who would know how to please him, would he be disappointed by her virginity? She found herself hoping quite strongly that he wouldn't.

Returning to her empty bed-sit late that afternoon was an anticlimax. Having gone so far, she wanted to carry on and get everything over with. But her life had been switched to hold, suspended. All she could do now was wait for the other shoe to drop.

It was Friday evening before it did.

After a succession of practically sleepless nights, Mia was tired out, yet at the same time keyed-up and restless, waiting for Sander to ring. It was almost impossible to believe that tomorrow was to be her wedding-day.

Or perhaps it wasn't. Maybe Sander had never intended to go through with the wedding. Maybe the whole thing had been just a cruel hoax on his part. Then the recollection of his look when he'd said, 'I want you more than I thought it possible to want any woman, and I mean to have you,' made her know she was wrong.

Unable to settle to anything, she had a bath, then gave herself a shampoo and a manicure. She was in her white towelling robe, brushing out her long damp hair, when the bell rang.

It would be Trevor come to call her to the phone. Hurrying to the door, she pulled it open, the words spilling out. 'I'll need just a moment to get dressed...'

'There's no need to bother on my account. I much prefer you as you are.'

Hardly able to believe her eyes, she found herself looking into Sander's strong, dark face. Her heart stopped, then began to race unevenly.

Though annoyed by her own weakness, she'd soon given up the struggle not to think about him, and he'd been on her mind constantly. Now she gaped at him as if the sheer weight of thoughts had conjured him up.

'Your mouth's open,' he informed her, green eyes glinting between thick lashes. 'It's a very nice mouth, and it's giving me ideas I can't indulge while we're standing on the doorstep.'

Mia fell back in disarray and he followed her inside, closing the door behind him.

'W-when did you get home?' she asked, still retreating.

'About an hour ago.' The reply was abstracted. He was looking at her in a way that made her toes curl inside the fluffy mules.

'So you've come straight from the airport?'

'Yes.' His voice deep and husky, he added, 'But to hell with standing here making polite conversation— come and give me a kiss.'

Pride told her she ought to make some effort to dissemble. Desire, however, proved too strong. She went to him, lifting her face, shiny and free of make-up, with undisguised eagerness.

His mouth claimed hers with a sweet hunger that gave her the curious sensation that she was weightless, floating. When eventually he freed her lips, wanting more, she clung to him, pressing herself against him.

Gripping her upper arms, he held her away a little, commenting with a crooked smile, 'It seems that absence *does* make the heart grow fonder! Is that by any chance an invitation, Mia?'

She wanted to say yes, to take the last irrevocable step and pre-empt tomorrow. But the knowledge that the fuel which fed the fire was lust, not love, held her back.

When she bent her head without answering, Sander put a finger beneath her chin and lifted her face to enable him to read her expression.

'No?' He sighed. 'Ah, well, I suppose that's just as well. If I once started making love to you, we might be still in bed tomorrow when we should be in church.' Smiling a little, he put a cool finger against her warm cheek, causing her blush to deepen.

After a moment his eyes strayed to where the lapels of her terry robe had parted, giving a tantalising glimpse of creamy breasts. 'Perhaps you *had* better put on some clothes, or all my self-restraint will go by the board. Then pack what you want to take with you. You'll be staying the night at Crombie Square.'

In something of a daze, Mia gathered up a pair of navy cords and a blue and white knitted top, the first things that came to hand, and disappeared into the tiny bathroom. As soon as she'd scrambled into them, without bothering to put on any make-up she began to push everything she thought she would need into a soft-topped case. That done, she stood hesitating.

'Well, come along, woman!' Sander's voice was brisk, but held an underlying note of indulgence.

She felt bossed, taken over, yet she found the sensation wasn't altogether unpleasant. Anything was better than waiting in a kind of limbo, as she had been doing.

It was a beautiful evening, temperamental April in one of her most pleasant moods. The dusky air was clear and calm, still holding the sun's warmth; the sky an inverted bowl of deep blue, spangled with stars.

Once they were settled in the car, Sander felt in his jacket pocket, and lifting her left hand, slipped a ring on to her third finger. It fitted as if it had been made for her.

Mia stared at it in surprise. It wasn't the conventional diamond she might have expected had she envisaged having an engagement ring, but an unusual yellowy stone in a wonderful antique setting.

'What is it?' she asked.

'A sardonyx. The gem that denotes conjugal happiness.'

His words gave birth to an odd flutter of excitement which died as he added ironically, 'Our friends will undoubtedly expect some show of sentimentality.'

During the journey to Mayfair, Sander went over the wedding arrangements, ending, 'I've been in touch with your father and Miss Renshaw, so they both know what's happening.

'St Giles' is only a small church, and the ceremony will be a quiet one. Just a handful of relatives and a few close friends have been issued with invitations over the phone.'

Apparently as an afterthought he added, 'Is there anyone I might not know about that you'd care to send a last-minute invitation to?'

Mia shook her head, and, still ruffled by his earlier remark about sentimentality, said, 'What would I say? I'm marrying a man I don't even like, come and wish me joy?'

A muscle jerked in Sander's lean cheek and his long fingers tightened fractionally on the steering-wheel before relaxing again. After a moment, without looking at her, his voice curiously flat, he asked, 'Why *are* you marrying me?'

'You know why.'

Smoothly sarcastic, he said, 'I mean, why are you sacrificing yourself so nobly for a father who doesn't care two hoots about you?'

'He *does* care about me!' she cried. Then desolately, 'No, that's not true. He doesn't love me. He never has. Or perhaps he did until...'

'Until...?' Sander prompted.

'Until the car crash.'

'Go on.'

The accident was something she'd never spoken of, though the memory had haunted her for years and so had the nightmares.

'It was a motorway pile-up,' she told him after a moment, her voice scarcely above a whisper. 'My father, who was driving, escaped without a scratch, and I was only slightly injured. But my mother died and so did my twin brother...'

'How old were you then?'

'Just turned eight.'

Even at that tender age she'd been aware of her father's bitterness and despair at losing the son he had idolised. Faced with his unspoken but ever-present resentment, countless times she had wished that it had been the other way round and she'd been the one to die.

'Tell me about your childhood,' Sander said quietly.

Mia gave him a uneasy glance. 'There's not much to tell.' It wasn't a subject she cared to talk about.

'Your father didn't think of marrying again?'

'No, he never so much as looked at another woman. He buried himself in his work, while we had a succession of housekeepers, some nice, some not so nice.'

'It must have been very lonely.'

'Yes, it was,' she admitted shortly.

'But you had next-door neighbours, friends to play with?'

Mia shook her head. 'Our house stood in its own grounds at the edge of the Heath, and I wasn't allowed to go outside or have friends in.'

Her voice flat, holding not a vestige of emotion, she went on, 'I used to stand at the nursery window so I could see the other children playing. Sometimes when it was windy I used to watch them with their kites. I often wished I had a kite to fly.' For the first time she sounded wistful.

'Did you ever get to fly one?'

'No.'

'Where were you educated?'

'I had a tutor until I was eleven.'

Sander gave her a mock-threatening look. 'Do I have to use thumbscrews?'

Her expression stubborn, Mia said, 'I told you there wasn't much to tell.'

With a sigh he persisted, 'And after the tutor?'

'For the next seven years I went to a small private school for girls, and after that a secretarial college.'

'Then what?'

'As soon as I finished college I got a job with Rayfield's and left home.'

'Why? Surely you had no need to do either?'

Stiffly she said, 'I wanted my independence.' That was less that the truth. All she'd ever wanted was to be loved. But after all those years of trying to make up for Michael's death, of feeling guilty that she'd lived while he died, she couldn't take any more.

To her relief, Sander forbore to ask any further questions and relapsed into silence until they reached Crombie Square.

As they drew into the kerb a stocky, grey-haired manservant appeared and murmured a respectful, 'Good evening, sir, good evening, madam.'

'Evening, Thomas.' Sander tossed him the car keys. 'Will you put Miss Fielding's case in the guest-room and ask Mrs Rose to send a tray of tea upstairs?'

Having escorted Mia into the hall, Sander remarked, 'You've only seen the one room; let me show you the rest.'

Opposite the living-room there was a large study with book-lined walls. At the rear of the house, overlooking a walled garden, lay a long dining-room with french windows, and next to it was a cheerful airy kitchen.

Upstairs, double doors led into a central sitting-room with a door on either side. To the right was a pleasant bedroom decorated in maize and white and furnished in a light, modern style. Mia saw her case was already there, waiting on a low chest.

Throwing open the door on the left, Sander said, 'This is my bedroom, soon to be ours.' Seeing her gaze drawn to the king-sized divan, he queried, 'Which side do you prefer?'

That apparently innocent question tied her stomach in knots. Turning back to the living-room, she answered as levelly as possible, 'I don't actually know. I've always slept alone.'

He raised a sardonic brow. 'Really? Have *all* your lovers been men who had to hurry back home to their wives or fiancées?'

With something like despair, she protested, 'Thinking so badly of me, I don't understand why——'

'Why I decided to take you in hand? I enjoy a challenge.' Sounding a shade disappointed, he added, 'But I've gained the first two of my three objectives rather more easily than I'd imagined.'

'The first two?' she echoed.

'Making you want me, and making you marry me.'

Drawing a careful breath, she said tartly, 'May I know what the third one is?'

'Making you love me.'

That was the last thing she had expected him to say, and it shook her rigid. She half turned away and in a strangled voice managed, 'What difference does it make how I feel about you?'

Putting his arms around her, Sander drew her back against him and nuzzled his face into the side of her neck. 'All the difference in the world,' he replied softly.

Mia gave him a wary glance.

He smiled a little. 'Work it out for yourself.'

But she already knew. Loving a man like Sander would destroy all her defences, leave her wide open to any hurt he might care to inflict. A shiver ran through her.

She was standing imprisoned in his embrace, the breath caught in her throat, when, to her utmost relief, there was a tap on the door.

Sander released her and strolled to open it, remarking, 'This will be your tea ... Ah, thank you, Emily.' Having taken the tray from a small, round-faced maid, he turned to Mia and suggested, 'You look tired; why don't you drink it in bed?'

She stood staring after him while he carried the tray through and set it on one of the bedside cabinets. Returning, he kissed her on the lips, a lingering kiss that completed the rout. 'Goodnight—pleasant dreams.'

He was gone before she could say a word.

As soon as her brain and limbs would function again, Mia unpacked her toilet-bag and night things and cleaned her teeth in the adjoining bathroom. Then she climbed into bed and drank her tea, her thoughts wheeling about like a flock of disturbed birds.

Tomorrow night she wouldn't be sleeping alone. She knew a heart-stopping excitement at the thought of what her wedding night would bring. Sander had remarked that she wouldn't find it any hardship to share his bed, and it was the truth.

Though it was also the truth that there was more to marriage than sex. Much more. She was taking a dreadful risk marrying a man who, while he wanted her, despised her.

It was no use telling herself that she had no option. Of course she had. She could tell Sander to go to the devil. But what if he carried out his veiled threat to ruin her father?

He was certainly capable of it, yet somehow she doubted he would. He was betting on her giving in without a struggle, and if the gamble failed she couldn't see him being petty or vindictive enough to take revenge.

But she could be quite wrong. After all, how well did she know him? The truth was she hardly knew him at all . . .

She was being an utter fool, she berated herself. What chance had such a marriage of succeeding? It was odds-on that nothing but misery lay ahead. If she had an atom of sense she'd get up and leave now.

But she couldn't. He was like a fire in her veins, a fever in her blood. She might be taking a terrible risk in marrying him, but it was a risk she *wanted* to take...

Dawn was fingering the sky, and in the garden a thrush was singing his heart out, before she finally fell asleep. Sheer exhaustion catching up with her, she slept like a log until after nine, and only awakened when Emily arrived with a breakfast tray.

'It's a lovely day, miss,' the girl said, opening the curtains to let bright sun pour into the room. 'You must be getting all excited.'

When Mia had managed to smile and agree that she was, Emily, clearly a romantic, sighed and departed.

Mia poured herself a cup of coffee and, going to the window, looked out over the garden. Still sparkling with morning dew was a sweep of smooth green lawn edged by mature trees. Beyond the trees a paved walk wended its way between flowerbeds and bushes to a round white Victorian gazebo. A folly perhaps, as, surrounded by greenery as it was, it had no view.

Feeling a sudden chill that was due more to nerves than cold, she climbed back into bed. The breakfast Emily had brought up looked both dainty and delicious, but Mia was unable to eat a thing.

She was propped up in bed drinking her second cup of coffee when Sander, heart-stoppingly attractive and virile in fawn trousers and a black cotton-knit shirt, strolled in.

Stooping, he kissed her briefly—but proprietorially—before dropping a flat leather box into her lap. 'The groom's present to the bride.'

Hands not quite steady, she used a pale, shiny thumbnail to press the catch. It sprang open to reveal a collar of perfectly matched, lustrous ivory pearls.

Before she could begin to thank him, he said abruptly, 'When we're married I don't want to have to watch you or wonder where you are when you're not with me. I'd like your word that everything is over between you and Measham. That you don't intend to see him again.'

It was days since she'd given Philip a thought, and she knew with a feeling of sharp regret that she hadn't wanted to be reminded of him now.

Her grey eyes clouded, she asked slowly, 'And will you take my word?'

'Yes.'

'Then I give it.'

He nodded, as if satisfied. Turning to go, he said over his shoulder, 'I'd like you to wear your veil back when you go to church.' Though phrased as a request, it was undoubtedly an order. 'I want to see the look in your eyes while you're making your vows.'

Startled and disconcerted by his words, Mia could only sit staring after him, wondering exactly what he'd meant. It was a minute or so before she was able to gather herself and get out of bed.

A glance in one of the luxurious fitted wardrobes revealed her wedding-gown hanging shrouded in clear plastic, and, alongside it, Janet's dress and all the accessories neatly assembled.

She had just showered and put on her robe when Janet arrived, her thin face flushed, her brown eyes sparkling with excitement. In one hand she carried a small make-up case, while a handbag and a number of other packages dangled from the other.

'Well, here I am,' she said, 'your self-appointed bridesmaid. Sander sent a car for me, so don't I feel important!'

'You are important,' Mia told her. 'Without you, I might never be ready in time.'

The next hour fairly flew until, perfumed, powdered, and titivated, both the bride and the bridesmaid were ready.

Pale yet serene, the collar of pearls around her throat, the coronet set on her gleaming ash-blonde head, Mia stared at herself in the full-length mirror and, for perhaps the first time in her life, *felt* beautiful. While, flushed and smiling, pretty as a picture in her own finery, Janet made one last adjustment to the veil.

A knock heralded the delivery of the flowers. The bride's bouquet was a mass of creamy, scented freesias and lily of the valley, the bridesmaid's a posy of pink rosebuds and stephanotis.

James arrived a few minutes later, looking handsome and distinguished in a grey morning-suit with a white carnation in his buttonhole. After standing silently surveying his daughter, he cleared his throat and said a shade awkwardly, 'You make a beautiful bride.'

Janet went to the window and, bubbling with excitement, announced importantly, 'The bridesmaid's car's here!' Picking up her posy, she headed for the door, pausing only to threaten, 'If you're more than a couple of minutes late I might be tempted to marry him myself!'

It was a lovely day, the air sun-drenched and golden as, after the short drive to St Giles', Mia left the car on her father's arm. Though outwardly she appeared to be calm and confident, inwardly she was a quivering mass of nerves as they walked up the path to the old grey church set among budding trees.

James, apparently deep in thought, had scarcely spoken. Now he gave her a smile and, squeezing her hand, said gruffly, 'Today you look just like your mother.'

His words, and the unexpected gesture of affection, made her grey eyes fill with tears.

Janet was waiting just inside the porch. Smiling mistily, she took her place behind the bride.

The church was beautiful, full of flowers and organ music and the smell of incense. Sunlight slanting through the stained glass made a kaleidoscope along the tops of the polished pews and down the strip of red carpet which lay on the woodblock floor.

At the altar the Reverend Mr Jenkins, Sander, and a nice-looking, fair-haired stranger, clearly the best man, waited.

Obeying a given signal, the organist changed to the traditional wedding march, and, as a man, the twenty or so people in the congregation rose and turned to watch the bride walk up the aisle.

Most of them Mia had never seen before. Two she knew well—Rhoda, striking in a buttercup-yellow outfit, and by her side, Philip in a light blue suit.

Their eyes met, and Mia saw his expression change from curiosity to incredulity, then to a white mask of shock and anguish. Philip had come to see Sander married, but clearly he'd had not the faintest idea that *she* was to be the bride.

CHAPTER FIVE

MOMENTARILY Mia faltered, then somehow she tore her gaze away and kept walking.

Sander, a tall, handsome stranger in his grey morning-suit, was watching her. Just for an instant something primitive flared in his eyes, then all trace of emotion was wiped away, leaving his lean, dark face expressionless.

At the chancel steps she turned to hand her bouquet to Janet, whose look sent a heartfelt message of sympathy.

Her face cold and stiff, Mia took her place by Sander's side. Feeling oddly detached, as if her mind was standing apart from her body, she breathed in the scent of freesias and listened to the priest, balding and benign, as he began the lovely, solemn words of the marriage service.

'Dearly beloved, we are gathered together here in the sight of God, and in the face of this congregation, to join together this Man and this Woman in holy Matrimony...'

It was very quiet in the church, as if everyone present held their breath, so quiet that while the ceremony progressed she could clearly hear the distant hum of traffic on Park Lane.

The Reverend Mr Jenkins was an ordinary-looking man, but he had a most beautiful, resonant voice and he spoke the words of the old service with authority and real meaning.

'Wilt thou have this Woman to thy wedded wife . . . and, forsaking all other, keep thee only unto her, so long as ye both shall live?'

'I will,' Sander answered firmly.

Having expertly collected Mia's attention the clergyman proceeded, 'Wilt thou have this Man to thy wedded husband . . .'

Shaken by a strange regret, she thought, if only this were going to be a different kind of marriage, a marriage built on a foundation of love . . .

She turned her head and, taken unawares despite his warning, found herself looking straight into Sander's eyes. But she wasn't guilty of the promiscuity he suspected her of and, as far as she was able, she would keep her vows. Her own eyes clear and steady, she answered, 'I will.'

'Who giveth this Woman to be married to this Man?'

When James had played his part, Sander took Mia's hand and each gave their troth.

With due solemnity the best man produced the ring and laid it on the book, then to Mia's surprise put a larger, heavier ring beside it.

A strange feeling of warmth mixed with excitement tingled through her. Sander had chosen to wear a ring!

Almost immediately the warmth died. Of course it was for *show*. When he'd first told her that to take his father's place as head of the bank he needed to be married, hadn't he used the term, *respectably* married?

The priest handed Sander the smaller of the two wedding bands and he slipped it on to her third finger. 'With this Ring I thee wed . . .'

Her hands like ice, Mia put the other ring on Sander's finger and they both knelt.

'Those whom God hath joined together let no man put asunder. Forasmuch as Sander Christian and Mia Charlotte have consented together in holy wedlock . . . and have declared the same by giving and receiving of a Ring, I pronounce that they be Man and Wife together . . .'

After the register had been signed, Sander slid Mia's engagement ring back on to her finger to join the plain gold wedding band, before lifting her hand to his lips.

Though she felt sure the gesture of homage was just show, her heart did a strange flip and her knees felt weak and shaky.

The ceremony over, the organist broke into triumphant Mendelssohn. Her hand through Sander's arm, Mia smiled at her father, and at William, fresh-faced and portly, then, looking neither to right nor left, walked to the church door.

Waiting outside was an official photographer, plus several from the Press who had apparently got wind of the wedding. A wealthy banker marrying by special licence, and to a woman no one on the social scene had ever heard of, was news.

Photographs taken, bells pealing, the newly-weds were showered with rice and rose petals as, hand in hand, they ran down the church path.

To Mia's surprise, a carriage drawn by two white horses was waiting. Sander helped her up and, as soon as she had arranged her full skirts, took his place beside her. The groom chirruped gaily to the horses, held his whip, with its bow of satin ribbon, aloft, and they were off at a spanking pace.

As they clip-clopped through the sunlit streets, Press photographers running alongside, Sander put an arm lightly around her shoulders and stroked her neck with his fingertips. The caress sent little shivers running down her spine and totally took her mind off the pursuing reporters.

When they reached the house the door was standing wide, and the staff, comprising Mrs Rose, Emily, and Thomas, were waiting to greet them.

On the threshold, Sander paused to have a quiet word with the pressmen, who, to Mia's untold relief, promptly melted away.

The bridal pair were no sooner inside than the cars began to draw up and they had to turn to welcome their guests.

After several unfamiliar faces came William, who shook hands with Sander before kissing Mia heartily. He was followed by the best man, whom Sander introduced as Jon Ross, a long-time friend and colleague from the bank.

Jon was fair-haired, just above medium height and stocky, with hazel eyes and a square, rather serious face that lit up when he smiled. He took Mia's hand and said with engaging friendliness, 'Sander's a lucky cuss. You're everything he said you were!'

And then, too soon for Mia, Rhoda and Philip were advancing on them.

As she met Rhoda's look, Mia's mouth went dry and her throat constricted. There was fury and malice in the other woman's sherry-coloured eyes, a set determination to make trouble.

'What a surprise, coz!' she cried, appearing tiny and innocently doll-like beside the two tall men. 'When I got the message that you were getting married today I had no idea it was to our *femme fatale* . . .'

So Sander hadn't told Rhoda his plans.

Her lips twisted into the semblance of a smile, the redhead went on, 'I didn't know you two had got to know one another *that* well . . .'

Mia kept a smile pinned in place, and seeing Philip's fair face flush, willed him not to show his feelings.

'Tell me, how did you manage to pull it off so quickly?' Rhoda's words seemed to be addressed to Sander, but her swift glance made it obvious, to Mia at least, that the last question was meant for *her*.

But Sander was answering easily enough, 'I can move fast when my future happiness is at stake.'

Looking at the bride, Rhoda cooed, 'Well, I *do* congratulate you, you clever thing. You are *so* lucky!'

Mia stood like a statue while Philip kissed her cheek and shook hands with Sander.

As they moved away, Sander looked after them, his clean-cut face wearing a slight frown, before, a smile taking its place, he turned to greet the next couple.

The wedding breakfast, laid out in the dining-room in the form of a cold buffet, was very good, but Mia had no appetite. She sipped a glass of wine, and then another, while she smiled and talked and tried to look the epitome of a happy bride.

It was a great relief when the single-tier cake had been cut and the toasts made and answered. She was standing by Sander's side feeling light-headed and almost sick with nervous tension, when Rhoda suddenly appeared at her elbow, as beautiful and poisonous as an oleander.

'Well, finding you were our bride *was* a surprise, not to say a shock,' she said with saccharine sweetness. 'Even Philip had no idea . . . I'm afraid the poor boy was dreadfully upset by the way you simply walked out on him . . .'

Feeling like an inexperienced player trying to field a hand-grenade, Mia said guardedly, 'Well, I was certain Janet could cope. She knows the job as well as I do.'

Rhoda's sherry-coloured eyes glittered. 'She might know the job, but I doubt very much if she could take *your* place. I know Philip's never regarded you as just a secretary. In fact . . .'

At Sander's warning glance, she paused and changed direction. 'But everything seems to have happened so *suddenly*. When the note arrived telling us about the wedding and sounding so *mysterious* about it, I presumed it was Jacqueline he was marrying. They've been *close* friends for some time now. As close as you and——'

'Whoops, sorry!' Coming up from behind, Janet had jogged Rhoda's arm, almost spilling her drink. 'By the way,' Janet added, 'Philip was looking for you a moment ago.'

After a baleful glance, Rhoda ignored her and returned to the attack. 'What time are you *lovebirds* leaving for your honeymoon?'

'I don't really . . .'

As Mia faltered, Sander answered, 'In about an hour.'

'Where are you planning to spend it?'

'I'm keeping our destination a secret,' Sander told her blandly.

Mia heard his words through a kind of muffled roar. She felt hot and nauseous, and her head had started to spin muzzily. 'If you'll excuse me,' she said, and headed blindly for the french windows.

Once outside in the fresh air she felt a little better. Needing to be alone and quiet, she crossed the lawn, her skirts sweeping the cropped grass, and headed through the screen of trees and bushes to the small white gazebo.

Inside it was cool and dim. Careless of any possible dust, she sat down thankfully on the semi-circular

bench and, leaning back, closed her eyes. Gradually
the sick emptiness went and her head began to clear.

In retrospect it seemed ridiculous, but, though
Sander had said, 'family and close friends,' she'd
never thought of Rhoda and Philip being there, or of
what their reaction might be.

Philip had clearly been stunned, shaken to the core,
but Rhoda had looked almost beside herself with rage.
Was it because she believed that Mia had somehow
managed to get *both* the men she'd wanted?

Knowing she couldn't stay away too long, Mia was
bracing herself to return to the house when the scrape
of shoe leather told her that Sander had come looking
for her. She opened her eyes, and with a shock of
surprise found Philip staring down at her.

'Oh, God, why did you do it?' he asked in a
wretched voice. 'Was it just to get back at me? If only
you'd waited I could have worked *something* out.'

'I don't——' Mia began.

But Philip was going on, 'I can't bear the thought
of you being married to some other man. How *could*
you marry him when it's me you love?' he added
thickly.

Seizing her upper arms, he pulled her to her feet
and, before she could protest, began to rain kisses on
her upturned face. With a passion she hadn't known
he was capable of, he cried, 'I won't let you go—I
won't! You're mine!'

'That's where you're wrong.' Sander's voice was like
a douche of icy water, making them spring apart. He
stood just inside the doorway, dressed now in a grey
lounge suit, sinewy and powerful, dangerous as a
wounded tiger despite the civilised garb. *'She's mine.*
If you come within a mile of her again, I'll break
your neck. I feel tempted to do it anyway.'

The softly spoken threat held a menace that made Philip blench.

Without looking at Mia, Sander ordered, 'Go and get changed.' His tone, though quiet, cut like a whip.

She glanced helplessly from one man to the other. 'But I don't want you to——'

'Your concern for your lover is so touching that I'm tempted——' Sander went on with a kind of raging calm.

'Oh, please, Sander... You won't...?' She broke off, realising that her obvious anxiety for Philip, who looked no match for such an opponent, was only making things worse.

Taking a deep, steadying breath, she brushed past the tall figure almost blocking the doorway, and hurried back to the house.

Though Sander was furious, he was a sophisticated man who could exercise self-control. He wouldn't upset his family and friends by beating up a guest at his own wedding. Or would he?

As Mia made her way between groups of laughing, talking people, saying, 'I'm afraid it's time I got changed,' to the ones who would have detained her, Janet appeared. Taking one glance at Mia's ashen face, she practically hustled her across the hall and up the stairs.

'You look as if you've had more than enough—and no wonder! I nearly *died* when I saw Rhoda and Philip in church. I gather they didn't know it was *you* Sander was marrying?'

'No, they didn't.'

'Rhoda looked fit to be tied. By the way, sorry for butting in, but I thought she was going to spill the beans about you and Philip and cause a scene.'

'So did I,' Mia admitted.

Frowning, Janet asked, 'How *did* she get to know? I don't suppose Philip...?'

Mia shook her head. 'He wouldn't have told her. It would have made things far too awkward for everyone. But as soon as her birthday party was over he was intending to break the engagement.'

'So why didn't he?'

'Before he could, Rhoda announced that she was going to have a baby.'

'I see.' Janet whistled. 'So he was sleeping with her? Men are the giddy limit!'

As she began to help Mia out of the rustling wedding-dress she went on, 'But if Philip didn't tell her about you, I wonder how she found out?'

'The same way that you did?' Mia hazarded wearily. 'Though we always tried to be careful *not* to look at each other when she was there.'

'Too careful, perhaps?' Janet suggested, her brown eyes shrewd.

'Possibly. Or maybe it was pure intuition on her part. As things have turned out, I just wish for everyone's sake that she didn't know.'

'You can say that again! You'd think having got her own man back she'd be satisfied, but she's clearly out for blood...' Janet sighed. 'When I first got to know her I thought she was quite nice, but she's being an absolute bitch.'

'You can't blame her,' Mia said heavily. 'First her fiancé, then a man she...clearly regards as special.'

'I *can* blame her,' Janet contradicted stoutly. 'She has a wicked tongue. Though she got no change out of Jon Ross when she hinted that one of the reasons you'd married Sander was for his money. He looked at her as if she'd crawled from under a stone and said very quietly, ''Mia strikes me as a lovely, genuine girl, and I've never considered Sander to be a fool''...

Anyway, take my advice,' Janet went on, 'don't let what's happened this afternoon throw you.'

Having put the wedding-gown on its hanger, she trotted off downstairs while Mia changed into her going-away outfit.

Dressed in the lilac-blue silk suit, she took a look at herself in the mirror and frowned. Her brows and lashes were several shades darker than her hair, and normally her skin was clear and creamy without being too pasty, so she needed very few cosmetics. But now, in spite of the carefully applied make-up, she looked dreadfully pale. Still, perhaps 'wedding-day nerves' would account for that.

Janet's advice, 'Don't let what's happened this afternoon throw you,' was more pertinent than the other girl had realised. Mia sighed, her stomach churning with anxiety. Yet somehow she had to carry on as if nothing had happened, at least until she and Sander were alone.

But where *was* Sander? Was he so angry he'd decided to call off the honeymoon?

The door opened and Janet was back with the bridal bouquet. 'You look marvellous,' she said sincerely. 'All ready for the big send-off? Come on, then, don't dawdle—the cases are in the car, Sander's waiting, and the worst's over.'

That was where Janet was wrong, Mia thought bleakly, as the door closed behind the other girl.

The hall was crowded with guests, and at the foot of the staircase Sander waited. Holding the bouquet, head high, a smile on her lips, Mia descended the steps and took the hand he held out to her.

'You look delightful,' he said, and gave her a charming smile, but there was no warmth in his handsome eyes.

As he drew her into the hall she caught sight of Rhoda and Philip in the middle of a group at the far side. After a quick glance which seemed to confirm that Philip was unharmed, Mia carefully avoided looking their way.

She hugged her father, and William, and blew a kiss towards Janet and Jon Ross, who were standing together. Then, showered once more with rice and rose petals, she and Sander made for the waiting car.

He opened the door, and she turned to throw the bouquet before getting in. Her aim was good, and Janet caught it easily. When Mia was settled in her seat Sander got behind the wheel and, having returned the waves and smiles, they were off.

They drove out of London towards Heathrow without speaking a single word. Now the need to keep up appearances was over, Sander was looking aloof and unapproachable.

'You haven't told me where we're going yet,' Mia ventured after a while.

'We're catching the evening flight to Hong Kong.' He answered with a frigid politeness that was more off-putting than anger.

Seeing Hong Kong had been a lifelong dream, and Mia would have been delighted if things had been different. All she could feel now, however, was anxiety over what had happened.

Somehow she had to find the courage to talk to him, to explain that she hadn't broken her promise, that what must have appeared to be a tryst was actually nothing of the kind.

In a small voice she began, 'Sander, I . . .'

He turned his head and looked at her with such coldness that the words froze on her lips. With a heart like lead she relapsed into silence. How could anyone penetrate that icy reserve? Perhaps if she waited a while until his anger had had time to abate...

Mia's experience of travelling by air had been limited to a couple of cramped economy-class package holidays, and on both occasions she'd felt claustrophobic and unaccountably nervous of flying. But this time, having so much on her mind, she boarded the huge jet without a qualm, and was amazed at the first-class space and luxury that greeted her.

The first leg of the journey was into darkness, and after an excellent dinner most of the passengers settled back to rest. Sander, though wide awake and with a smile and a word for the attentive stewardess, was, as far as Mia was concerned, a civil but uncommunicative stranger.

Feeling headachy and miserable, she closed her eyes and tried to sleep. But, weary though she was, she was unable to relax, and dozed only in fitful snatches.

Just after dawn the jet refuelled at Dubai for the second part of their journey. Except for tantalising glimpses of mountain ranges and jungle as they flew over India and Burma, this leg of the flight was as uneventful as the first.

They were nearing their destination when the evening meal was served. Since leaving Heathrow the food had been superb, but Mia had scarcely eaten a thing.

Now, her appetite non-existent, she had started to refuse the proffered tray when Sander intervened smoothly, 'You must eat something, darling, even if it's only to please me.'

The stewardess's glance said plainly that in Mia's place she'd do anything to please him.

Eyes glinting, he went on, 'I prefer to beat my wife rather than starve her into submission.'

Smiling at his joke, the stewardess moved on.

Half convinced he meant it, Mia shivered, feeling even less like food. But somehow, under his watchful eye, she managed to force down part of it.

As they approached Kowloon it was still light enough to make out that just off the mainland there were countless islands scattered in the South China Sea. Some were rocky, others flat and lush and green, edged with sandy beaches.

On the mainland, the New Territories lay to the north, a quiet patchwork quilt of rice fields and small terraced farms, while Kowloon, a mass of twinkling lights, hugged the shoreline. To the south was Hong Kong Island, its Victoria Peak rising higher than the tallest skyscrapers.

Generally regarded as one of the most spectacular in the world, the landing at Kai Tak took them low over the canyon-like streets of Kowloon. The final approach was made between tall buildings, and what seemed to be merely feet above a wide and busy road.

Mia caught her breath, trying to control the sudden fear that threatened to swamp her. Sander's left hand was lying loosely in his lap. Needing the reassurance it seemed to offer, she reached out blindly and took it. She had hoped it would close around hers, but it didn't, and as soon as they had touched down it was withdrawn.

She glanced at him. For an unguarded moment his green eyes stared straight into hers, and the look in them shook her rigid, making her heart race with alarm.

Such a long journey, she had hoped and believed, would help to dissipate his wrath, but in that instant she saw it had had precisely the opposite effect. Contained, his fury had built up like pressure inside a volcano, until it threatened to explode.

Now it was too late, she wished despairingly that she had forced herself to explain straight away rather than leaving him to think the worst. But she had held back partly, she admitted now, out of cowardice, fearing that he might not believe her. Grimly she faced the fact that now he was even less likely to believe her.

All through the journey Mia had longed for it to be over. Now it was, dreading the moment she would have to face up to Sander's anger, she wished it could have been never-ending. Though surely, in the confines of a hotel room, furious as he was, he would be bound to maintain a certain degree of control?

Outside the main terminal building the night air was hot and humid. Though the place was seething with a multitude of people, within seconds Sander had secured a taxi.

The driver, brown and wizened as an old walnut, stowed their luggage in the boot before taking his place behind the wheel. A hand-rolled cigarette dangling from the corner of his mouth, he darted in and out of heavy traffic with an abandonment which argued either great faith that his illustrious ancestors were watching over him, or a wish to join them.

After the third near-miss, Mia protested, 'You couldn't ask him to go more carefully?'

Unmoved, Sander replied, 'He *is* going carefully by Hong Kong standards.'

They drove towards the harbour through Kowloon's crowded, colourful streets, with their multitude of garish neon signs. Having taken the under-the-harbour tunnel which joined mainland Kowloon to Hong Kong Island, they negotiated Hong Kong's flat Central district, and began to climb, leaving the bright lights and busy streets behind them.

Finally, in a quiet, dark, tree-lined road, the taxi drew up outside wrought-iron gates set in a high, pale stone wall.

Carrying one of Mia's cases, Sander opened the gates and, a hand on her elbow, led the way through the lush greenery of a semi-tropical garden.

No lighted windows shone through the dusk, and, sudden apprehension making her voice sound thin and high, she remarked, 'This doesn't look much like a hotel.'

'It isn't a hotel. This is where I live. Or rather, where I used to live.'

The house was a flat-roofed, split-level place built of honey-coloured stone and hidden from the road by riotous vegetation. Squashing down an insane desire to pull free and run, Mia allowed herself to be shepherded along a paved terrace at the rear.

From the terrace, sliding glass panels led into a large lounge which was blessedly cool, with the minimum of light, modern furniture and lots of books and green plants. Beyond the lounge, through a white archway to the right, was a dining area, and behind that a well-fitted kitchen. To the left lay a master bedroom and a guest-room, each with its own luxurious bathroom.

Having opened the doors and shown her round in silence, Sander went back to take care of the rest of the luggage and pay the driver.

Striving for normality, Mia unpacked her night-clothes and toilet things before going back to the lounge. Then, with a sense of mounting panic, she sat on the couch and waited for his return and the confrontation that was certain to follow.

CHAPTER SIX

THOUGH Mia was waiting for Sander with fixed intensity, she didn't hear him return. Some sixth sense made her look up, and a shock-wave jangled along her nerve-ends to find he was standing in the doorway watching her through narrowed green eyes.

As she rose to her feet he took a deliberate step or two towards her. There was no mistaking the anger, the intense hostility in every muscle of his tall, powerful frame.

She stood her ground, wanting to run, but doubting very much whether her legs would carry her. In any case, where was there to run to?

'Well?' The softly spoken word was a challenge, a gauntlet thrown down.

'I didn't break my promise,' she denied above the wild clamour of her heart.

He looked at her, his mouth grim, his eyes full of unconcealed antagonism.

'Or at least I didn't intend to——'

'Don't bother lying to me,' he interrupted curtly.

She struggled for calmness and found at least a semblance of it. 'I'm telling you the truth. I didn't feel very well... Perhaps I'd drunk too much wine on an empty stomach. All I wanted was to have a breath of fresh air and a few minutes alone——'

'When I got there you weren't alone. You were in another man's arms, kissing him.' His icy rage shattered her hard-won composure like a flying pebble shattered glass.

'I wasn't kissing him. *He* was kissing me. I didn't want him to...' Head bent, the light throwing the shadow of her long lashes on to her pale cheeks, Mia stopped, unable to say another word for the tears that choked her.

After a moment Sander said flatly, 'You look exhausted. Do you want to go to bed?'

She fought down the cowardly urge to say yes, and shook her head. 'I...I'd like to talk to you first. To explain about Philip.'

'I don't want you to "explain". I'll settle for some hard facts.' Seeing her sway on her feet, he ordered, 'And sit down before you fall down.'

Pushing her into the nearest chair, he towered over her. 'You told me you loved him... How long is it since he first said he loved you?'

She swallowed. 'About four months.'

'How often did you meet?'

'Not often... When we could.'

Contempt in his voice, Sander said, 'I take it that Measham hadn't got the guts to face up to things, to break the engagement and put his job on the line.'

'It wasn't like that. At first he didn't want to hurt Rhoda. He was fond of her.'

Ignoring Sander's look of derision, Mia went on, 'Finally he told me he couldn't go on as we had been doing. He said he'd made up his mind to break the engagement, but he didn't want to do it until after Rhoda's party. Then, when he got there that night, he found she was pregnant.'

'Pregnant?' For a moment Sander looked startled, then his lip curled. 'So he was sleeping with her while he carried on his affair with you.'

'We never had an affair,' she protested. 'Not in the way you mean. We never slept together.'

'Oh, come on,' Sander said tightly. 'You surely don't expect me to believe that?'

'It's the truth.'

'You're forgetting that night in the garden—the night you thought I was Measham. Your response was so eager, so passionate that, to use a modern idiom, it blew my mind. You're also forgetting I *heard* Measham say, "It's me you love. I won't let you go... You're mine".'

Mia shook her head. 'He didn't mean——'

Ignoring her protestation, Sander demanded, 'What made you agree to such a cosy little ménage à trois? Were you afraid of losing him altogether?'

'I didn't agree to it. I would never have agreed to it... I had no idea they were... lovers until——'

'Until you found out that he'd got her pregnant and was going to have to marry her,' Sander finished grimly. 'I see.' Then, like a knife-thrust, 'So you did marry me just to get back at him?'

'No! No, of course I didn't.' Somehow it *mattered* that he believed her. Desperately she added, 'You *know* why I married you.'

He looked unconvinced. 'You could have told me to go to hell. Did you really believe I'd ruin your father?'

No, deep inside she hadn't believed it, and she found herself unable to lie.

'Well, *did* you?'

Seeing he was intent on having an answer, she said, 'I believed you were ruthless enough.'

As if sensing the unspoken qualification in her reply, he pressed, 'So there was some other reason?'

She hesitated, not knowing what to say.

'You weren't fool enough to think you could get away with carrying on with Measham behind my back?' Before she could find her tongue, he went on,

'Rhoda thinks you only married me as a cover to do just that. Not very flattering to me, but she might be right.'

'She *isn't*,' Mia protested. 'She just wanted to cause trouble.'

'It seems to me that you're the one who's caused all the trouble. But then you've always been jealous of Rhoda, haven't you?'

'Did she tell you that too?'

'Isn't it true that you were jealous of your father's fondness for her even before Measham came on the scene?'

Though Mia had always fought to stifle the feeling, the accusation was so close to being the truth that a painful flush suffused her face.

'There's no need to answer,' Sander said drily. 'Is that the reason you did your level best to take Measham away from her? Sort of tit for tat?'

'What kind of woman do you think I am?' she cried.

He laughed shortly. 'I know what kind of woman you are. The kind who, despite her promise, cuckolds her husband by sneaking off to meet another man while she's still wearing her wedding-dress.'

Grey eyes luminous with unshed tears, Mia denied vehemently, 'I didn't *plan* to meet him. He must have followed me. I never intended to——'

'Make a fool of me?' Sander broke in roughly. 'But that's exactly what you have done, and I don't allow anyone to do that and get away with it.' A cold pride was in his face, hooding his eyes and emphasising the autocratic flare of his nostrils.

Mia's chest filled with a tight knot of pain. After a moment she whispered, 'So what do you intend to do? Have the marriage annulled?'

'Do you imagine that would make me look any less of a fool?' At her involuntary movement, he said, 'Of course it wouldn't. Quite the contrary. Tell me, sweet wife, what do *you* think I should do?' When she stayed silent he asked mockingly, 'Run out of answers?'

Without consciously deciding what she was going to say, she found herself asking, 'The vows you made in church yesterday—did you intend to keep them?'

His eyes narrowed to gleaming green slits, but he answered, 'Yes.'

'I intended to keep mine.' Ignoring his raised eyebrow, she ploughed on, 'I still do, if only you'll give our marriage a chance.'

'For better or for worse?' he asked ironically.

'Yes,' she said, very low. Then more strongly, 'Perhaps we can make it "better" if we both try.'

'Very well, dear wife.' Taking her wrists, he pulled her to her feet with a swift jerk. 'Having been disillusioned about one thing, let's see how you perform in bed.'

Shocked by the anger still simmering just beneath the surface, she begged miserably, 'Please, Sander——'

'I'll do my best,' he promised. 'Presumably frequent and exciting sex was one of the things you married me for. I'll endeavour not to disappoint you.'

His smile cruel, he added, 'If Measham was trying to keep both of you satisfied, with Rhoda having prior claim, there must have been times when you were very disappointed.'

He was deliberately setting out to hurt her. But if she backed out now—supposing he would allow her to—there was no hope at all of saving their marriage.

But when he pulled her against him, suddenly afraid of all that male strength unsoftened by love, she stiffened, panic beginning to claw at her, and tried to pull away.

An arm like a steel band clamping her to him, he forced up her chin and kissed her with a fierce passion that beat down any attempt at resistance and made her head reel.

His mouth still covering hers, he swept her up into his arms and carried her through to the bedroom. He tossed her on to the bed with an almost contemptuous disregard for her as a woman, and began to unbutton his silk shirt.

Her heart pounding at an alarming rate, Mia wriggled off the bed and stood up. At his sharp glance she stammered, 'I . . . I need to go to the bathroom,' and fled.

As the door closed behind her, she resisted the temptation to push home the bolt. Though a small one, at that moment it represented some degree of safety. But she couldn't take refuge in the bathroom all night. If she tried to, he'd either break down the door and take her by force, or ridicule her assertion that they could make their marriage work.

When she'd showered and cleaned her teeth, Mia picked up the clothes she had put over a chair. Common sense told her it would be stupid to get fully dressed again, but at the same time she couldn't bring herself to walk back in there naked. Donning just her lacy undies, she stood trying to bolster her spirit enough to return before Sander came looking for her.

But all at once she felt sure that if she stayed in the bathroom all night he wouldn't do that. Having shown her how he intended to behave, he was forcing her to make the final decision.

She hesitated, afraid of the violence she had aroused in him. Yet she could hardly go back and, like some novelette heroine, plead, 'Be gentle with me'. Stifling an almost hysterical desire to giggle, she opened the door and went into the bedroom.

Though Sander was in bed it was obvious he'd used the other bathroom. His thick dark hair was curling a little, still damp from the shower, and, knowledgeable enough to know what damage bristles could do to her delicate skin, he had shaved his hard, lean face.

He was lying indolently, his hands clasped behind his head, his broad chest bare, a fine cotton sheet drawn up to his waist.

As she hesitated, he asked caustically, 'Are you intending to sleep in your undies?'

'No, of course not.' Her voice cracked a little.

'Then take them off.' It was a command.

Hands icy cold, Mia obeyed, and, feeling his eyes running over her nakedness in critical appraisal, reached hastily for the nightdress that she had put on the bottom of the bed.

'You won't be needing that,' he told her sardonically. 'Though tonight is our wedding night, I'm not in the right mood to want to take it off.'

Throwing open the bedclothes, he invited, 'Get in,' adding with soft violence, 'And for God's sake stop looking as if you're frightened to death of me!'

'It's not that,' she said with only partial truth, trying not to stare at his magnificent body. 'Only this isn't how I imagined our——'

Her words ended in a squeak as, with a sudden, impatient movement, he pulled her on top of him. His hands one each side of her rib-cage, he raised her so that the tips of her breasts brushed his chest, which was lightly covered with dark curly hair.

It was unbearably erotic, or so she'd thought until he lifted her higher and took one of her pink nipples into his mouth, his tongue coaxing it into firmness before he began to suck and tug gently.

She gasped and shuddered, shaken to the depths of her being by the storm of feeling he aroused. Even though he was angry, she realised dimly, he wasn't intending to just use brute force and satisfy himself.

In fact quite the opposite. By the time he had leisurely explored and enjoyed every part of her body and was ready to take her, she was almost mindless, half sobbing with the desire he'd aroused, all fear of his hurting her totally forgotten.

Even so, his first powerful thrust made her cry out and try to repulse him, until the need for fulfilment washed over her again and her arms went around his powerful back.

But her body's instinctive reaction seemed to have thrown him, and, though she arched beneath him, pressing herself against him, it was a second or two before he began to move again, this time with care until her movements matched the rhythm of his. Then, with the driving power of unleashed passion, he brought her to a climax so intense that she thought she would die.

For a while she lay with her eyes closed, quivering uncontrollably. Then his weight lifted from her and he rolled away, leaving her cold and bereft. She opened her eyes to find him lying with his smooth, golden-skinned back to her, and felt such a sense of rejection that she was unable to hold back the tears.

Perhaps she made some slight sound, because he turned, and, with a muffled oath, pulled her against him, cradling her head against his chest. 'Don't cry,' he said roughly. 'I didn't mean to hurt you.'

But she was crying not because he'd hurt her, but because her encounter with Philip had spoiled what could have been a blissful wedding night.

She fell asleep with the tears still wet on her cheeks.

Some time during the night Mia awoke. She was lying close to Sander's side, her head pillowed on his shoulder, her hand spread on his flat midriff. She moved slightly, nestling even closer, unaware that he was awake until he asked softly, 'Want something?'

She'd thought the fires of passion were, temporarily at least, doused, but they were only banked, as his expert touch soon proved, and they flamed into life at once.

Turning on his side, he drew her back against him and, his hands caressing her breasts, once more dragged her down into a wild, tumultuous whirlpool of delight. This time she was more aware of *his* passion—the hiss of his breath, the heavy thumping of his heart, the groan he gave as he shuddered against her.

Next time she surfaced it was to find the pleasant room full of late morning sun. Pushing back the tumble of ash-blonde hair, she turned her head to find Sander lying quietly, watching her.

He had eyes of the most fascinating shape and colour, she thought dreamily, eyes that would have made even an ordinary man unforgettable, and he was far from ordinary.

She stretched and, becoming aware of a bodily satisfaction she had never known before, smiled lazily at him.

He was all she had ever wanted or dreamt of in a lover, warm and masterful, skilful and passionate, sensitive and tender despite his tough exterior.

Then, as she suddenly recalled the scene that had led up to his lovemaking, her grey eyes clouded.

His jaw tightened. 'Just realised it's the wrong man in bed with you?'

'I've never been to bed with Philip, or anyone else for that matter.'

'It's a pity you didn't try telling me so more forcefully. Then I wouldn't have hurt you.'

'Even if I had, I doubt if you'd have believed me.'

'Probably not,' he admitted shortly. 'Though I always felt there was something that didn't quite fit.'

Strangely disappointed, after a moment she ventured, 'I thought you'd be pleased.'

'I'm delighted,' he told her emphatically, 'if a little puzzled. You told me you loved him; why *didn't* you sleep with him? Don't tell me he didn't want you to!'

'Yes, he wanted me to, but I couldn't . . . It seemed so sordid, deceiving Rhoda like that.'

'But he was deceiving you if he was sleeping with her while he was swearing it was *you* he loved.'

'I don't want to talk about Philip.' She didn't even want to think about him.

As if reading her mind, Sander asked, 'How much does the thought of him bother you?'

'How much does the thought of Jacqueline bother you?' she flashed—then wished she hadn't mentioned the glamorous model.

'Touché,' Sander accorded. Then abruptly he asked, 'Why didn't you tell Measham you were marrying me?'

'Why should I? Everything was over between us. What I did had nothing to do with him, and he would have——'

'Tried to talk you out of it?'

She nodded, adding ruefully, 'I never thought of his coming to the wedding.'

'I never thought of your slipping off to meet him.'

So he still didn't believe her.

Pride wouldn't allow her to deny it again, so she set her teeth and said nothing. But unconsciously her fingers plucked at the sheet, betraying her agitation only too clearly.

Sander sighed, then, as if deliberately pushing the clouds away, stretched like a sleek cat and asked, 'Well, woman, are you going to get up, or what?' The sudden gleam in his eyes left no doubt as to what the 'or what' was.

Still shy, and unwilling to admit she wanted to stay, she stuck her small nose in the air and informed him loftily, 'I'm getting up.'

She was out of bed before it occurred to her that she was stark naked. Snatching up her négligé, she pulled it on, and headed for the bathroom, aware that he was amused by her confusion.

Her body ached pleasurably, and instead of showering she ran a bath. She was stretched full length in the warm, scented water when the door opened and Sander strolled in.

Casually dressed, he was carrying a steaming cup of tea, which he put down on the flat side of the bath. Then, with all the arrogance of a sultan, he stood looking down at her, inspecting her slender body, the obvious signs of love, with a glint of satisfaction that brought a surge of colour into her face.

Only when she grew really uncomfortable and restive under his scrutiny did he take pity on her. Heading for the door, he said over his shoulder, 'Breakfast in about ten minutes.'

In the doorway he paused, and sighed elaborately. 'So much for being a husband, a man with rights. Here I am slaving over a hot stove while my wife wallows like a contented hippo!'

He moved quickly, and the sopping sponge she threw at him hit the closed door. She heard his soft laugh as he walked away, and her heart seemed to turn right over.

If only things had been different. If only he'd loved her, instead of just marrying her to keep her out of Rhoda's way and because he needed a wife. But he didn't love her, and all the 'if onlys' in the world wouldn't make an iota of difference.

When she'd finished drying herself, Mia put on a simple cotton dress with ties at the shoulders and, doing her best to look cool and self-possessed, went through to the lounge.

The house was most pleasant, decorated in pastel shades which gave a feeling of airiness and space. It was the abode of a man who liked to move about with ease and freedom, who preferred his living to be stylish but uncluttered.

Outside it was hot but a little less humid than the previous evening. At the rear the ground dropped away sharply, and the sunny terrace looked over a wooded slope and hanging gardens to a distant sprawl of roof-tops. A full cooked breakfast was set out on a table beneath a fringed umbrella, and there Sander was waiting.

He pulled out a chair for her. Taking her place at the table, Mia sipped a glass of cool orange juice appreciatively while Sander helped her to thin slices of ham and an egg. Finding an unexpected appetite, she was tucking in with gusto when all at once the incongruity of it struck her. 'How on earth . . .?' she began.

Sander laughed, making his eyes sparkle and showing the excellence of his teeth. 'A Chinese couple, Lily and Empha Chan, live close by, and between them they look after the place for me. Empha's pride and joy is the garden, while his wife cleans, shops, and cooks.'

'So you weren't slaving over a hot stove?' Mia accused, as she buttered a piece of toast.

'You sound disappointed,' he observed with a grin. 'But as it happens, I was. I told Lily that, apart from seeing the place was ready for us, she needn't come in except to tidy up and get an occasional evening meal. I thought someone else being in the house might inhibit us.'

The softly added rider, and what it implied, put a tinge of pink into Mia's cheeks.

Satisfied that he'd disturbed her, Sander poured coffee for them both and asked idly, 'Do you consider Hong Kong a good choice for a honeymoon?'

'I . . . I don't really know. Though I'm sure there must be plenty to do.'

His eyes glinted wickedly. 'Would you say having "plenty to do" is a prerequisite for newly-weds?'

Determined not to be teased, she gave him a cool glance and said composedly, 'There's a limit to the amount of time even honeymooners can spend in bed. They need something else to do.'

'Care to bet?' he murmured.

The way he was looking at her from beneath the long, thick lashes which almost brushed his high cheekbones made her heart flip crazily. He was practically irresistible.

Jumping to her feet, she went to lean on the parapet. A warm breeze lifted the pale, heavy silk of her hair and tinkled through hidden wind-chimes.

Sander followed and stood behind her, his hands running up and down the soft flesh of her upper arms. Mia gazed unseeingly at the beauty spread before her, conscious only of the man touching her with such casual possessiveness.

Bending his dark head, he nuzzled aside her hair and feathered his lips across her nape, making a shiver run through her. Then, folding strong arms around her, he drew her back to rest against him, his arms crossed, his thumbs just touching the underside of her breasts. It was like a powerful electric shock, leaving her paralysed, unable, even if she'd wanted, to protest or move away.

He followed the curve of her shoulder and neck up to the delicate whorls of her ear with his lips, before turning her to face him. His kiss was sweet, tantalising.

Softly he said, 'Though of course we can go out if you'd like to.'

As he spoke Mia found herself watching his face, his mouth. *Oh, that mouth . . .* Liquid fire began to course through her veins.

'Come on,' he said with a remote kind of mockery.

'What?' She dragged her gaze away from his mouth to look into those brilliant eyes.

'Come back to bed. You know you want to.'

'No,' she denied huskily, trying, for the sake of her pride, to hold out against him.

Sliding his fingers into the silky fall of hair to hold her head, he drew her closer, brushing her mouth sensuously with his own, the tip of his tongue outlining her lips, coaxing them to part for him.

Pulling away, she protested breathlessly, 'You said we could go out.'

His arms imprisoned her again. 'So we can. Afterwards.'

As though punishing her for that abortive attempt at resistance, Sander displayed his domination by skilfully playing with her until she was a mindless, quivering mass of sensations.

It was some considerable time later, after being made love to until, unable to stand any more of the exquisite torture, she was forced to beg for mercy, that he let her go and headed, naked, for the bathroom.

Feeling drained and exhausted, yet at the same time content and pleasurably sated, Mia lay for a while watching the patterns of sunlit leaves moving on the cream ceiling, before making an effort to get out of bed.

After a refreshing shower, she put on a yellow and white striped cotton shirtwaister and joined Sander in the comfortable lounge to await the taxi he'd phoned for.

'Did you have your own car when you were living here?' Having a husband was still new to her and, a little embarrassed by what had gone before, she felt the need to make conversation.

Well aware of her reason for asking, he smiled, but answered all the same, 'No. Having a car in Hong Kong is just a liability. All kinds of public transport are still good and frequent, and if I needed a car any time I hired one.'

As he finished speaking, the sound of a horn announced the arrival of their taxi.

'Are we going anywhere special?' Mia wanted to know, as they got out of the cab at the Hilton Hotel in Central, Hong Kong's banking and business district.

'I thought I'd take you up Victoria Peak,' Sander told her.

Looking after the departing taxi, Mia hazarded, 'So we need to walk up?'

Sander shook his dark head. 'We could have gone in the cab. The Peak is one of the most sought-after residential districts on the Island and there's a good road which winds right to the top. But I decided it would be more fun to take the Tram.'

The terminus for the Tram, which was actually a funicular railway, was a mere hundred yards or so behind the Hilton Hotel.

It was a spectacular ride. The Peak rose an impressive five hundred metres above the harbour, and there were five stations en route where passengers could be picked up or set down. As they climbed steeply upwards through the trees, Central's skyscrapers fell away and to the right an airy panorama opened up.

At the top, the impressive Peak Tower, culminating in a cream, boat-shaped structure rising high above the surrounding building, was thronging with people.

As they strolled through its complex of shops and kiosks, pausing first to watch some finger painting, then the ancient art of jade carving, Mia suddenly stiffened. Just ahead of them was a tall, slimly built man with expertly styled blond hair. While she stared at him, her heart in her mouth, he turned his head, presenting a handsome, boyish profile.

Mia let out the breath she had been unconsciously holding. It wasn't Philip, nor was the resemblance nearly so marked as it had at first appeared.

She glanced covertly at Sander, to find him watching her, a thin white line of fury drawn around his mouth.

'I . . . I thought . . .' she stammered.

'I know what you thought,' he said harshly. 'You must have spent every minute secretly brooding over Measham when you conjure him up from the first tall, fair man you see.'

'You're quite wrong. I haven't even——'

Before she could find the words to convince Sander that he was mistaken, his anger was under control and he'd changed the subject by asking coolly, 'Ready for lunch?'

They took the lift up to the Tower's oval restaurant. Perched like an eyrie, it gave magnificent views over the north shore of the Island, the harbour, and across to Kowloon.

Having ordered, Sander helped Mia to some delicious seafood salad served on a bed of crushed ice and, as though determined to forget what had gone before, began to tell her about Hong Kong.

She was listening to his low, attractive voice, watching his face, with its well-marked brows, its strong bone-structure, and firm yet sensitive mouth, when, glancing up, she became aware that she wasn't the only woman hanging on his words.

He made an impact on most females, his sheer masculinity hitting them with the force of a prairie wind. But there was no need for the platinum blonde a couple of tables away to ogle him quite so openly, Mia decided crossly.

Nor, having noticed the overt interest, was there any need for him to look back with such calm appraisal.

A thought, prickly as a dried holly leaf, stabbed her. Surely she couldn't be...? No, of course she wasn't jealous, she told herself sternly. It was ridiculous to feel so vexed, so *possessive* just because another woman was making it more than plain that she fancied him.

As Mia lifted her chin, Sander's eyes, specks of gold sparkling in their green depths, smiled into hers, taking her breath away. There was a mocking little twist to his lips and she had the uncomfortable sensation that he knew exactly what she was thinking and feeling.

'Surely I know you?' Leaving with her good-looking young escort, the blonde had paused and, ignoring Mia completely, was leaning across the table, giving Sander an eyeful of cleavage. She was a beautiful woman, exquisitely dressed and turned out, but considerably older than Mia had first thought.

Sander rose to his feet courteously.

'I'm Rebecca Manders,' the vision added. 'I'm sure we met on the slopes at St Moritz in February.'

Coolly polite, Sander answered, 'I'm afraid you're mistaken. I haven't been skiing in years.'

'You weren't at St Moritz?' The blue eyes widened innocently. 'Then it must have been somewhere else. I never forget a face.' Especially such a striking one, her glance added.

When Sander said nothing, she went on, 'My husband's in Macao on business, and I get very lonesome while he's away, so tonight I was thinking of having a small party on our yacht, *Aphrodite*. Perhaps you'd care to come?'

Her meaning couldn't have been plainer, the invitation more blatant.

'It's very kind of you to ask us,' Sander said smoothly, 'but I'm afraid both my wife and I are a little tired. A honeymoon can turn out to be quite strenuous.'

The blonde's carmine lips thinned. Turning on her heel, she rejoined her escort and headed for the door.

With just the faintest flicker of distaste, Sander resumed his seat and his interrupted meal.

Mia gave an inward sigh of relief. He had been so annoyed over what he had obviously seen as her obsession with Philip that she'd half wondered if he would deliberately encourage the blonde. Now she felt ashamed of thinking such a thing. Sander was a mature, well-balanced man, not a raw adolescent who would indulge in childish tit for tat.

Over the next week they saw and did as much as they could fit into the hours at their disposal. For Mia, each outing became an exciting treat, and she found herself looking forward eagerly, not only to the day ahead, but to sharing it with Sander.

Amongst other things, they roamed around the Sung Dynasty Village, took a boat ride to Lantau to look at the houses built on stilts, and climbed, through a straggle of tin-roofed huts and singing bamboo, the five hundred steps above Sha Tin to see the Monastery of Ten Thousand Buddhas.

Catching a tram to the old fishing town of Shakeiwan, they strolled through the colourful streets, ate dim sum—various small Chinese delicacies steamed in round bamboo baskets the size of tea-plates—and went to the zoo.

Sander was laughing at the antics of some chimps when, noticing a small boy struggling to see, he hoisted him out of the crowd and settled him on one wide shoulder. He seemed to like children, and they liked him, Mia found herself thinking. He'd make a good father.

As each day went by, she was learning something fresh about this complex man who was her husband. She had discovered that he was capable of pity without sentimentality, and kindness without condescension. He was disciplined without being dull, discriminating without being fastidious, and romantic without being what Janet would have termed 'soppy'.

Because of his imposing size, his raw male magnetism, she had at first thought him something of a rough diamond. He looked tough, and undoubtedly was, but now she knew that he was also dangerously polished, a clever, cultured, sophisticated man, yet a man able to appreciate and enjoy the simple pleasures offered by a trip to the zoo.

Most evenings, after showering away the dust of the day, they went up to the Eagle's Nest, on the top floor of the Hilton, for cocktails, then on to sample a variety of restaurants and nightclubs before going home to make sweet, exciting love.

Mia had believed that what she felt for Sander was just physical attraction, pure chemistry. But now she realised it was more than that. Much more. It was a kind of strange passion which grew stronger with each passing hour until it was almost an obsession.

She was constantly, heart-stoppingly aware of him. The thought of his lovemaking was always just beneath the surface of her mind, and, though she thoroughly enjoyed their days, she waited for the delight the nights brought with an eagerness she found hard to disguise. He only had to look at her to heat her blood, only touch her to have her body crying out for him.

CHAPTER SEVEN

ONE night, having made love until dawn, they slept late next morning and, at Sander's suggestion, set off without breakfast.

'Tell you what,' he said quizzically, 'if you find you're getting hungry I'll buy you a McDonald's Special.'

Mia returned his grin. 'Ah, gee, thanks!'

'That accent is terrible,' he complained.

'I'll work on it,' she promised.

Intending to go to the Jade Market in Kowloon, they walked the mile or so to the Star Ferry. Having passed through crowded turnstiles at the harbour, they boarded the green and white *Morning Star* to make the short, breezy trip across one of the busiest and most romantic stretches of water in the world.

A lot of the passengers were tourists, and the ones carrying cameras were soon snapping the famous waterfront, not unlike that of Manhattan, with its massing skyscrapers pointing glass fingers of ice-blue and bronze into the scurrying sky.

Standing by the rail, an arm around Mia's waist, Sander advised, 'Look to your left.'

Sailing towards them over the sparkling water was a junk, stark and dramatic, picturesquely sombre with its bat-black sails.

She caught her breath, inexplicably moved by that strangely haunting vessel. A glance at Sander's face made her oddly convinced that he was too, despite his inscrutable expression.

110

Leaning against him contentedly, she admitted that everything about this husband of hers pleased her. She liked his insight and understanding, his love of beauty and order, the keenness of his intellect and his positive approach to life.

The brief crossing over, they spent what was left of the morning strolling around the fascinating Jade Market, where every inch of space was awash with a greenish sea of gemstones.

Towards one o'clock, Sander asked, 'Ready for a spot of lunch?' and, when she nodded, surprised her by steering her towards a back-street food stall. Sitting beneath a sagging bamboo awning at one of the rickety tables set out on the dusty pavement, they used chopsticks, which Mia had quickly become expert with, to eat bowls of steaming white rice topped with pink prawns and green and red peppers in a piquant sauce.

A small sloe-eyed girl in white silk trousers brought a pot of jasmine tea, which Sander declined in favour of beer.

'It's very refreshing,' Mia remarked, having sipped at the scented, straw-coloured liquid.

He grimaced. 'I'm happy to say I've never acquired a taste for something so reminiscent of bathwater!'

The simple meal finished, they took a ferry back to the Island and followed the tourist route along Hollywood Road and Ladder Street, where everything under the sun was displayed in the exotic setting of an ad-hoc Asian emporium.

Coughing, Mia lit joss-sticks at Man Mo temple, red and smoky as hell itself with its sacred fires and enormous coils of burning incense. Then, while Sander looked on approvingly, she fed all their loose change into a box for the poor, before they started off down yet another narrow alleyway with open doors leading to dark interiors.

Passing one such doorway, partly curtained with sacking, Mia wrinkled her nose and muttered, 'There's a very odd smell.'

Sander grinned. 'Probably the local opium den.'

They were climbing a narrow, stepped street, half in bright sun, half in deep shadow, when he paused outside a small, dim, open-fronted shop hung with scrolls and charts, strange symbols and astrological signs, and said, 'I'd like to go in here.'

The words were spoken casually, but they held an underlying purpose, and Mia realised he had brought her this way with that very thing in mind.

Putting an arm loosely around her shoulders, he drew her inside.

A girl with a cap of shining black hair cut into a straight fringe across her forehead, and jet black Oriental eyes, was sitting behind a table covered with cards, books, and circular star maps.

With a polite, but unsmiling gesture of greeting she said to them in good, sing-song English, 'I am Anna... You wish me to tell future? What the stars hold?'

Mia had begun to shake her head, when Sander said gravely, 'I would like to know if the prospects for a certain match are propitious.'

'Match between yourself and lady?'

'That's right.'

Mia was standing a little in the background. Taking her hand, he drew her forward.

She felt a distinct reluctance, a strong impulse to turn and hurry out of the shop. Somehow, illogically, what the Chinese girl might be about to tell them *mattered*. If the prognosis was against the match, she didn't want to know.

Sander spanned her wrist with his fingers and said in her ear, 'I thought you might enjoy a spot of local colour.'

Mia felt an odd relief. 'Then you don't really care what the forecast is?'

'Oh, yes...' his voice was softly adamant '...I care.'

A price was agreed on and paid in advance.

Anna waved a small, fine-boned hand. 'Please to sit down.'

They sat side by side on three-legged stools.

Pulling forward a wad of charts, Anna explained, 'I find special characteristics of birth years, then make match. Each year must be compatible with other to make good match. You understand?'

'We understand,' Sander answered levelly.

Turning to Mia, Anna said, 'Please to tell day of birth?'

Her voice not altogether steady, Mia said, 'I was born on the twentieth of April.'

'Please to tell year of birth?'

When Mia had told her, Anna nodded and consulted her charts. 'That is Year of Dragon. Female born in Year of Dragon thinks free, is loyal friend, has good health, care for personal appearance, by working hard makes much achievement. Female born in Year of Dragon is sensitive, insecure, secretive, hides passions hot as dragon breath beneath armour cool as dragon scales.'

There was a silence, then Anna lifted her gleaming black head and looked at Sander. 'Please to tell day of birth?'

'December twentieth.'

'Please to tell year of birth?'

He complied.

'That is Year of Snake. Snake is good sign, beautiful sign. Much misunderstood by many people. Male born in Year of Snake has power, charm, charisma to attract opposite sex. Male born in Year of Snake is wise, self-disciplined, guards well own privacy, is strong, faithful, protective of loved ones.'

Anna placed the palms of her childish hands together as though in prayer, and stared down at a circular chart.

It was idiotic that it should matter so much, but, with a hollow sensation in the pit of her stomach, Mia held her breath.

For the first time, Anna smiled, showing small, pearly teeth. 'It is fortunate. Dragon and Snake deal well together. I make a highly favourable match.'

The tension which had been gripping Mia snapped like an overstretched rubber band, leaving her feeling almost dazed.

She heard Sander thanking the Chinese girl and pulled herself together enough to add her own thanks, and to hope that he hadn't realised how strongly she had been affected.

'You know what struck me?' he remarked, when they were outside once more in the dust and heat of early evening. 'Our English stars are compatible as well. Aries and Sagittarius are both fire signs. We *do* make a well-matched pair.'

As they emerged on to the main street, he raised a hand and, with the slickness of a magician performing a well-rehearsed conjuring trick, had a red and silver taxi drawing up beside them in an instant.

When they got back, Mrs Chan, a small woman, thin and sallow-skinned, her hair and eyes coal-black, her smile shy, was already in the kitchen preparing dinner.

'I've a business call to make, then I'll ask Lily to fix us a long cool drink,' Sander said, and disappeared inside, while Mia, her feet still protesting at the amount of walking she'd done on hot pavements, flopped into a lounger on the terrace.

Impatient night having elbowed lingering day aside, dusk had fallen swiftly, and the sky was a deep blue velvet spangled with stars. A warm breeze carried the heady perfume of flowering shrubs and trees and myriad spicy scents of the Orient, and mingled them with faint swirls of pungent smoke from the Moon Tiger mosquito coils.

If she lived to be a hundred, Mia thought, she would remember this smell. No matter what happened in the future, whether or not the prediction came true and they 'dealt well together', it would always take her back to Hong Kong, to her honeymoon and Sander.

He was a complicated man and, despite their growing closeness, still something of an enigma. Why had he asked about the prospects for their marriage? And why had she found that the answer mattered so terribly?

From their very first meeting there had been a magnetic pull between them, the attraction of opposites. Fair to dark, slim daintiness to power and strength. An attraction which, from the word go, she had struggled to fight, not fully realising that it wasn't only physical, that a far more potent force was at work. A force that had filled her heart and mind, taken her over body and soul. She'd called it passion, an obsession, never love.

But that was what it was.

Mia felt a rush of pure joy. She *loved* Sander. She wanted to cry it aloud, to shout it from the rooftops. To tell him, so he'd know that Philip meant nothing to her, and he needn't be jealous.

Don't be a fool, she scolded herself, of course he wasn't *jealous*. To feel that particular emotion he would have to care for her. But obviously all he felt was the possessiveness of any male animal for what he regarded as his female.

And, she realised abruptly, to admit her love was the very last thing she could do.

Like a bitter frost which shrivelled her joy, she recalled what he had said on the night before their wedding. 'I enjoy a challenge. But I've gained the first two of my three objectives rather more easily than I'd imagined . . . Making you want me, and making you marry me.'

She heard herself asking, 'May I know what the third one is?'

And his reply, 'Making you love me.'

Mia shuddered, and shuddered again. The thought of loving him, being his completely, would have been bliss if he had loved her. But he didn't. He'd started out by actively despising her. On his part it was mere lust.

An ugly word, she thought bleakly. A word which seemed to bear no relationship to what had passed between them, to the pleasure given and received.

Still, one thing was abundantly clear. If Sander knew she loved him, that knowledge would give him an even stronger hold over her.

But if he knew she loved *him* he would also know that Rhoda's interests were safe . . .

No, for her pride's sake she couldn't tell him. When his lust was sated and he tired of her—and perhaps, with his third objective gained and the challenge gone, he would lose interest that much quicker—she would mean less than nothing to him. A wife he no longer needed, a wife he could easily get rid of once the power at the bank was securely in his hands.

Yet when she had asked him if he meant to keep his marriage vows, he had given an unhesitating, 'Yes'.

Had he meant for life, or just for as long as it suited him?

There was a whisper of movement and he was lowering himself into a chair beside her. His glance seemed idle, to hold no threat, but behind that lazy regard she discovered an intensity that took her by the throat. It was almost as if he had guessed exactly what had been going through her mind.

After watching her for a moment or two in silence he asked softly, 'Do you believe in astrological predictions?'

When she hesitated, sensing a trap, he went on, 'I thought you might. Earlier you looked quite serious.'

She answered with caution, 'I ... I'm not sure that I do.'

'Ah, but are you sure you *don't*?'

'Well, I ... I don't think they can be dismissed entirely.' Only when it was too late and the words were spoken did she realise it would have been better to have said nothing.

Jumping to her feet, she went to stand by the parapet, her hands agitatedly gripping the smooth stone which still held the sun's warmth. Aware that Sander had followed and was standing close behind her, she gazed over the jewel-encrusted panorama without seeing a thing.

'Then you do have some faith?' he pressed.

'Some,' she agreed in desperation.

The trap snapped shut. 'You were very relieved when the match was compatible.'

It was useless to deny it. Feeling as if she was suffocating, she stood mute.

'So relieved it made me wonder if your feelings had changed.'

'I ... I don't know what you mean.'

'If perhaps I'd gained my third objective?'

'You haven't,' she denied, her pulses racing. 'I don't love you. I'll never love you.'

He pulled her back against the hard length of his body. She drew air in sharply as one hand moved across the bottom of her stomach, while the other lay just over her heart.

'What you mean is you'll never admit it,' he corrected. His voice holding a kind of silky menace, he added, 'Not unless I get tired of waiting, which I may well do, and force it out of you...'

There was a movement in the living-room behind them and Mrs Chan appeared, carrying a small tray which held two long drinks chinking with ice.

Mia's breath was released in a small sound almost like a sob.

'Reprieved,' Sander said drily. 'At least for the time being.'

The weather remained good and they made the most of it, taking daily excursions which kept them out from early morning until dusk.

Contrary to what Sander had said that night on the terrace, he seemed content to bide his time, making no attempt to force any admission from her. Finding there wasn't an immediate threat, Mia began to relax again. At least during the day.

The nights were a different matter. As well as the utmost pleasure, the nights brought apprehension. A fear that sooner or later she would betray her love.

Under the hot seduction of his mouth and hands she tried to remain silent, but found it impossible. In the extremes of passion he forced from her gasps and moans and feverish murmurs, but some small part of her mind managed to keep control and, as far as she was aware, she had said nothing coherent, given nothing away.

Thursday dawned hot and sunny. Having awakened quite early and made long, delectable love, it was mid-morning when they finally showered and dressed.

Sander had made no reference to its being her birthday, so Mia presumed he had forgotten. Trying not to feel disappointed, she waited until they'd had their orange juice and toast before asking, 'What are we doing today?'

'First a special lunch, then I've a birthday treat lined up for you. Luckily it's just the weather for it.'

He stayed secretive and silent as to what the treat was, while they walked through streets tiger-striped with sun and shade. A warm, boisterous wind was chivvying swirling dust-devils, fluttering flags and awnings, and whipping the blue-green water of the harbour into a million glittering crests.

In Central they made their way to the quaint Scarlet Warrior, and in the gaudy, theatrical atmosphere had a tasty lunch of spring rolls. Having wiped their hands on the steaming, scented towels brought to the table, they finished with bowls of sweet, refreshing lychees before setting off to take the Tram to Victoria Peak.

When they arrived at the top, Sander led Mia away from the built-up area and through the park, with its sub-tropical trees and plants, its neat paths and benches, to an open grassy stretch culminating in a rough knoll.

There, a makeshift wooden booth was hung with bunches of brightly coloured prancing balloons, nets full of glossy balls, gaily whirling windmills, and monkeys suspended by elastic from the end of sticks. Inside, nuts and popcorn, chocolate and lollipops, sweetmeats of all kinds jostled cans of fizzy drinks and tawdry souvenirs.

A weedy youth with pimples and a lank black fringe was in charge. He was friendly and smiling and lo-

quacious. When Mia remarked on the excellence of
his English, he told her proudly that he was Eurasian.

While a small boy clung to his mother's hand and
hopped excitedly from foot to foot as he watched his
name being stencilled on to a chosen balloon, Sander
walked Mia a few yards distant. Turning her to face
the shining sea, he instructed, 'Wait here, and no
peeping.'

The high wind, with its oven heat, flattened her
tangerine cotton skirt against her slender legs and blew
her hair into wild disorder. In the distance a man was
attempting to fly a model aeroplane and, closer, a
couple of laughing, squealing children were playing
with a frisbee while their parents lounged on a rug.

Sander was back quite quickly. From behind her
he said, 'Don't turn round, just lift your hand.'

Mia did as he'd instructed, and reaching over her
shoulder, he closed her fingers around a plastic reel
wound with cord, and advised, 'Hold on tightly.'

As soon as he let go she felt the pull and peered
upwards. There, soaring high above her in the blue
sky, was a snow-white kite. Happiness bubbled inside
her, fizzing and sparkling, shooting upwards, a newly
released fountain of pure joy. He'd remembered her
childhood wish!

She laughed aloud and began to run, the kite
plunging and rearing, tugging at its nylon tether like
a living thing. Only when she was breathless did she
flop on to the grass beside Sander, who had sat down
to watch her.

He was leaning on one elbow, his expression lazily
amused, but there was a look in his green eyes that
bespoke some much deeper, more powerful emotion.

Lying on her back on the warm turf, Mia wound
more nylon round the reel and, gazing up at the
swooping kite, tried to read the gold stencilling on it.

When she succeeded, her heart began to leap as dizzyingly as the kite had done. She'd expected it to be her name, or a birthday greeting.

What it actually said was, *I love you*.

If only it were true! If only he did love her... She turned her head to look at him, her gaze involuntarily questioning.

'When I mentioned we were on honeymoon, our young friend who, incidentally, rejoices in the name of Samson, seemed to think that was appropriate.'

Sander's dry comment left her faint stirring of hope stillborn and a leaden disappointment weighing her down.

She was endeavouring to recapture her earlier happier mood, when a red frisbee landed with a whoosh between them.

Smiling, Sander expertly skimmed it back to the waiting children, before taking Mia's free hand and pulling her to her feet. 'Come on, lazybones, let me give you a lesson in kite-flying.'

They spent the rest of the afternoon playing like carefree children, before walking back through the park to have a refreshing pot of tea. The wind had dropped considerably and they sat in the palm-shaded garden of the Rainbow Bird, lazily content to watch the world go by.

A huge red sun, temporarily defeated in its daily battle for supremacy, had slipped over the edge of the earth, and the evening rush of visitors to the Peak had started before they took the Tram down to Central.

'A taxi?' Sander asked.

Mia shook her head. The exercise they'd had that afternoon had been less tiring than walking about all day on hot pavements.

Quite unselfconsciously, he carried the kite tucked under his arm as they walked through the busy streets, the lights and neon signs making them brighter than day.

When they reached home they found the table had already been set with damask linen, flowers and candles, and a bottle of champagne was chilling in an ice-bucket. Mrs Chan was moving about, noiseless in her flat slippers, preparing an elaborate meal.

She put both her hands together in a gesture of supplication, and said in English, 'I hope you like. How soon you wish to eat?'

Turning to Mia, Sander queried, 'Do you want to shower first?'

'Yes, please. If it won't upset Mrs Chan's timing.'

'About half an hour?' he suggested to his housekeeper.

Lily nodded and smiled rather shyly before going back to her preparations.

Sander bent his dark head and his lips close to Mia's ear, asked enticingly, 'Shall we shower together? We could make it an exciting way to save water.'

Shivers running up and down her spine at the very idea, she answered breathlessly, 'I think I've had enough excitement for one day.' But, when he followed her into the bathroom and began to remove her clothes, she made no further demur.

She was convinced that standing beneath the jet of warm water while Sander soaped every inch of her slender body was the most erotic thing that had ever happened to her, until he handed her the soap and said, 'Your turn.'

She began at his shoulders, the smooth golden skin with its rippling muscles fascinating her, then down the broad chest with its sprinkle of dark curly hair. When she reached the taut stomach she faltered.

Though she knew the powerful male body well, she had never actually touched him, and a certain constraint made her hesitate to do so now.

She glanced up. The mocking challenge in his eyes told her he knew her feelings exactly.

Damn him! she thought, and, with a smile as old as Eve's, picked up the gauntlet. Her hands slid over the flat abdomen and moved lower, stroking and squeezing caressingly. She heard the hiss of his breath and thought triumphantly that she'd won.

Suddenly he caught her wrists and lifted her hands, placing them around his neck. Then, smiling, he cupped her buttocks and drew her close. Softly he said, 'This way we both win.'

When they finally emerged it was to find that Mrs Chan had placed all the food on the hotplate and left.

Having eaten her fill, Mia sat back with a sigh. 'Your Mrs Chan is a treasure.'

'I'll tell her you said so,' Sander answered gravely. 'She'll be pleased. Now you can relax on the settee while I get some coffee.'

They had drunk their second satisfying cup when he reached across to the wall unit and produced an oblong leather case. 'Your birthday gift.'

She opened the lid and gazed speechlessly at the pendant lying on the black silk lining. It was a four-centimetre oval of jade, clear and dark green as Sander's eyes, set in gold. Across it sprang a magnificent winged and clawed fiery gold dragon with moonstones for eyes. Intertwined with it, its gold scales matching those of the dragon, was an emerald-eyed serpent.

It was an exquisite piece of work, so perfect and appropriate that she knew he must have had it made to order. Her wits having totally deserted her, she gazed at it without knowing what to say.

'Of course, if you don't like it . . .'

'Oh, I *do*. It's wonderful!' She raised shining eyes.

'Then let me put it on for you.' He took the pendant and, lifting aside the smooth weight of ash-blonde hair, fastened the fine gold chain around her slender neck. It felt cool and heavy, unfamiliar and exotic against her heated skin.

'You have the most fascinating eyes I've ever seen on a woman,' he remarked. 'A true grey, no hint of blue, and with a dark rim round the iris that gives them clear delineation. Often they're a lucent silver, but when I touch you they turn dark and cloudy with passion.' Then, with no change of tone, 'Love me?'

Fire engulfed her and her heart began to race. All that was reckless in her cried out to say yes. Common sense fought the flames and doused them. Silently she shook her head and prayed he wouldn't force the issue.

He didn't. All he said was, 'Well, come to bed and show me how much you want me.'

On their last day, Sander suggested they take the bus to Aberdeen, a part of the island's coast they had never previously visited.

Leaving the hot, juddering vehicle with a crowd of locals, they walked to Aberdeen's packed harbour, where whole families—parents, grandparents, children, dogs, cats, even chickens and pigs—lived aboard the large, green-tarpaulin shaded boats. The scene, colourful and picturesque, could well have been the Orient of a hundred years ago.

Having bargained with a child-sized, buck-toothed lady, clad in what appeared to be floral silk pyjamas, who assured them, 'Husband row sampan good,' they took a trip around the harbour.

Seated on the wooden slatted bench which ran round the boat, Mia peered over the side and said in a heartfelt voice, 'I should *hate* to fall into that!'

'Can't you swim?' Sander enquired kindly.

Regarding the water, which looked thick and about the same colour as oily pea soup, Mia shuddered. 'I shouldn't think that's relevant. I imagine I'd die of something nasty before I had time to drown!'

The boat ride over, they stretched their legs, strolling to a quiet spot overlooking the motley scene. Sitting down on a large, smooth stone, Sander pulled her on to his lap, making her heartbeat quicken as it always did when he touched her.

A sea breeze blew strands of silky, sun-bleached hair across her cheek. He brushed them back, tucking them behind her ear. Then his lips followed the path of his fingers, lingering with a touch that could have been mistaken for tenderness.

That hint of tenderness was practically her undoing. She was filled with an almost overwhelming desire to put her arms around his strong neck and kiss him back. To tell him she loved him and beg for his love in return.

Was she mad? He had no love to give, nor did he want her love except possibly as a weapon to use against her.

'Enjoyed your honeymoon?' he murmured, his tongue tip exploring the warm hollow behind her ear.

Holding tightly to her self-control, she replied, 'I love Hong Kong; it's so full of life and colour.'

'That isn't precisely what I asked.' He sounded lazily amused. 'Are you sad our honeymoon's almost over?'

The true answer was yes, she wanted it to go on for ever. But it might not be wise to say that, she reminded herself.

'Well, are you?' he pressed, his lips following the clean curve of her jaw.

Summoning up her defences, she lied coolly, 'I won't be sorry to get back to London.'

'And to Measham?' Abruptly the amusement was gone.

'I won't be seeing Philip,' she said stiffly.

'But you still love him.' It was a statement rather than a question.

Her lips opened, then closed again, the denial unspoken. If he believed she still loved Philip it would safeguard her secret. After a moment she answered obliquely, 'Everything's over between us.'

'It had better be.' Sander's words were almost a snarl. 'If you lie to me again . . .'

Though he left the threat unfinished, Mia shivered, cold in the hot afternoon sun, and wished they were staying safely in Hong Kong where Rhoda and Philip were half a world away.

CHAPTER EIGHT

THEIR big jet took off from colourful Kai Tak in brilliant sunshine, the very air holding a furnace heat. Though scrupulously polite, Sander was uncommunicative during the long flight back. Since their trip to Aberdeen, he had been quiet and aloof, and, after their previous closeness, Mia found the change almost unbearable.

She'd tried to tell him that she hadn't meant what she'd said about returning to London, but it was too late; the damage was done.

His face impassive, he had listened to her stammered denials, but it was patently obvious that he didn't believe a word.

They came down through heavy cloud to a grey, wet Britain. Heathrow had its usual air of being the crossroads of the world, but despite the apparent confusion they got through the formalities with speed and efficiency.

Thomas was waiting with the car and drove them to Crombie Square through rain-lashed streets.

Mia had felt uptight and edgy, but, finding that Sander seemed, temporarily at least, to have thrown the devil off his shoulder, she started to unwind.

The sitting-room was glowing with well-applied elbow-grease, and vases of spring flowers were everywhere. Their album of wedding photographs and a pile of presents lay on the oblong coffee-table.

Sitting on the settee in front of a comfortable log fire, Sander pulled Mia down beside him and put an arm around her while they looked through the album.

At that moment they could have been any newly married couple in love and happy with each other's company, she thought wistfully.

Together, and still with that feeling of concord, they opened the presents, occasionally exclaiming or laughing over the more extreme flights of fancy, and laying bets as to how many more toastracks would make an appearance.

Mia was admiring a cut-glass rose-bowl when she saw Sander's jaw tighten and, with a sinking heart, guessed who it was from before she read, 'Rhoda and Philip' on the card.

'If you don't want to keep it...' she began hesitantly.

Sardonically he asked, 'Are you suggesting we send it back?'

'No, of course not... We can't do that.'

'Then do whatever you think fit.' Sander's voice was dismissive.

'Perhaps we could give it to Oxfam, or one of the other charities?'

Though he seemed to relax again, Mia sighed inwardly, annoyed at being reminded of things they would both sooner have forgotten.

During the following days they settled down to a home routine. On the surface it was easy, contented, yet it wasn't wholly spontaneous. Aware that the threads of happiness were terribly fragile, and even a small tear could ruin the delicate fabric, both, it seemed, were treading with care, neither so much as breathing Philip's name.

Mrs Rose was still taking care of the house, but, after consulting Sander, who gave her *carte blanche*,

Mia was doing most of the cooking, which she enjoyed.

When she had first broached the subject, Mia had been apprehensive, wondering if the housekeeper might be upset. However, Mrs Rose had seemed relieved. 'Lately my rheumatism's been playing me up something cruel,' she had confided. 'And there's only half the staff a house this size should have, so it's been a bit of a struggle.'

Sander, though thoroughly enjoying the world of big business and banking, wasn't a workaholic like James. He could, and would, delegate where possible. But with the take-over of power due in a few weeks' time he was working flat out, needing to go in at weekends as well as staying late most evenings.

When he was working, Mia usually cooked herself a light meal and ate it in the pleasant kitchen, then, having little liking for television, curled up with a book while she waited for him to come home.

One evening, on the spur of the moment, she went to Hampstead to visit her father. Recalling his unexpected gesture of affection on her wedding-day, his remark about her looking like her mother, she wondered if he might be lonely, might even be pleased to see her.

He wasn't, and she knew she'd been in cloud-cuckoo-land when she'd imagined that, after a lifetime, his feelings towards her might have changed.

'Sit down,' he said grudgingly, when Mrs Brendan, the sour-faced housekeeper, had shown her in.

'How are you?' Mia asked, sitting on the edge of an overstuffed chair, looking like the unwelcome visitor she felt herself to be.

'I'm very well.'

His colour, she noted, was much improved, and he seemed better in himself, perkier, if such a word could be applied to her father.

'A drink?' he suggested, rising to his feet.

She didn't want a drink, but she found herself saying, 'Please.'

Watching the stiffness of his movements as he went to the drinks cabinet, she was aware that he was as ill at ease as she was. They still had no point of contact. She'd been foolish to think otherwise.

Mia accepted the glass of pale dry sherry he poured for her and sipped it, feeling trapped. The large gloomy house was just as it had been when she'd escaped from it and, stifled by memories of the past, she couldn't wait to get away.

After some stilted conversation, mostly about work and the office, she was on the point of leaving when James demanded abruptly, 'I suppose you came expecting to be thanked?'

She looked at him blankly. 'Thanked? Thanked for what?'

He frowned, then, almost to himself, muttered, 'I made sure he must have done it for you.'

'Done it for me?' she echoed. 'I don't know what you're talking about.'

'In that case forget it.' James was plainly sorry he'd said anything, and more than anxious that she should drop the subject.

Mia rose to her feet and picked up her bag. 'I ought to be going. Sander will be home soon.'

Her father made no attempt to persuade her to stay any longer.

Uncomfortably she added, 'Well, take care of yourself,' and turned on her heel. It had been a mistake to come, she'd realised that from the start.

'Mia . . .'

Halfway across the hall, she paused and looked back.

His face uncertain, as though he would have liked to have bridged the gap, but didn't know how, James said, 'I hope you'll be happy.'

'Thank you.' Her eyes full of tears, she turned and kissed his cheek before letting herself out.

She'd been home almost half an hour when Sander got in. Having done quite a lot of thinking during the taxi-ride back and while she'd been waiting, she asked without preamble, 'What have you done about the money my father owes the bank?'

Sander finished taking off his jacket and loosened the knot in his tie before querying, 'What makes you think I've done anything about it?'

'I went to see him tonight. He was under the impression I'd gone to be thanked.'

'For what?'

Determined not to be beaten, she said, 'That's what I'm asking you.'

'Didn't you ask him?'

'Yes, but he refused to tell me.'

Sander gave her a sidelong glance. 'Suppose I refuse to tell you?'

'Then I'll have to draw my own conclusions.'

'And what might they be?'

'That somehow you've made things right, let him off the hook.' Wryly she added, 'I just hope you haven't cooked the books to do it.'

He threw back his head and laughed at that. 'It wasn't necessary to resort to cooking the books; happily I have plenty of money of my own.'

Before she could find the words to thank him, he asked, 'Ready for bed?' Sweeping her up into his arms, he added huskily, 'You have a very disturbing effect on me. During a most important meeting tonight all

I could think of was how soon I could get home and make love to you.'

Afterwards, lying in his arms and on the point of drifting off to sleep, she remembered. 'Sander...'

'Mmm?'

'Dad looked very much better tonight, as if the weight of the world had been taken off his shoulders... Thank you. I'm so grateful for what you did for him.'

'I didn't do it for him,' Sander answered shortly.

So he *had* done it for her. Did that mean his feelings towards her had changed, that he might be starting to care for her a little? Mia hugged the possibility to her like some precious gift.

A few days later, feeling she was cutting the last tie that linked her with her old life, Mia began to move her relatively few personal possessions out of the Bayswater flat. That done, she cleaned through for the last time and said goodbye to the other tenants before returning the keys to the agent.

It was then that she found herself at a loose end.

In the past, she had often felt she would make a natural lotus-eater, but now her only reservation about her new life was that she had so much spare time on her hands. After being a working girl, it wasn't easy to adjust to days of almost total ease. Shall we then find fault with paradise? she thought wryly.

When she told Sander how she felt, instead of dismissing or pooh-poohing her complaint as trifling, he listened seriously. Then, his green eyes thoughtful, he said, 'Well, unless you particularly want to, I'd rather you didn't get a job. As soon as my workload returns to normal I'd like you to be free to accompany me on trips abroad, or any spur-of-the-moment holidays.'

Having sent her winging up to cloud seven, he went on, 'At the same time, I don't want my wife to be bored. If you had your very own house to run...' He raised a questioning brow. 'Suppose we start looking for a place in the country?'

Though she was content enough at Crombie Square, Mia soared to cloud nine. 'A place in the country.' His words all at once gave this strange, unreal marriage credibility, even a sense of semi-permanence.

As she gazed at him, outwardly calm in spite of the excitement and joy bubbling inside her, he added, 'That should provide enough to do, at least for the time being. Perhaps you'd like to visit a few estate agents and see what they have on their books?'

With house-hunting to keep her happily occupied, the days suddenly weren't long enough. The nights never had been. Sander was an exciting, inventive lover, and, instead of lessening, her hunger for him grew. So did her love, until he filled her heart and mind and her very soul.

The only thing she needed to make her life as perfect as life on earth ever could be was for him to love her. For that she would willingly, happily have given up everything else, and thought it no sacrifice.

Sometimes, in the dark warmth of the night, lying in his arms, it seemed possible. In the cold light of day, she knew it was like wishing for the moon. But when he held her as if she were precious, looked at her with something that might have been tenderness warming his green eyes, she couldn't prevent herself dreaming.

On the following Thursday evening the phone rang. When Sander stayed at the bank late he usually gave her a call. Mia put down *So Long at the Fair* and reached for the receiver, hoping this might be him.

'And how is our little bride?' Rhoda purred.

Mia's instinctive reaction was to put the receiver back, but she conquered the craven impulse and managed coolly, 'I'm fine. How are you?'

'Oh, I'm quite well... But surely you're going to ask after Philip?'

'How is Philip?' Mia refused to be thrown.

'Missing you, apparently.' This time the venom was undisguised.

'I really don't think——' Mia began.

'Oh, he isn't *admitting* it. But he's very moody and unsettled.'

'Perhaps when you're married——'

'Darling, how naïve! Surely you of all people know that just because a man's married it doesn't mean he's going to settle down and be faithful. Take Sander, for instance...' Mia drew a short, sharp breath, while Rhoda went on, 'He's only been back from his honeymoon a matter of weeks and how many times has he already "worked late"?'

Teeth clenched, Mia refused to rise to the bait.

Getting no answer, Rhoda attacked from another angle. 'I suppose you know Jacqueline May is back in London?'

'That doesn't concern me.'

'Doesn't it concern you that Sander's meeting her nearly every night?'

'It might if I believed it.' Mia tried to sound airy, while a knife blade twisted painfully in her heart.

'Oh, you can believe it. Bentham's is known to be Miss May's favourite spot to dine. I dare say if you took a taxi there now you'd find them together.'

How certain she sounded! 'Was that what you rang to tell me?' Mia enquired evenly.

Hiding her chagrin well, Rhoda said, 'Actually, I called to ask if you were coming to the wedding. I was checking the replies and can't seem to find one from Sander.'

An invitation had come through the post, but, after glancing at it, he'd tossed it to one side. Unwilling to stir up a potential hornets' nest, Mia hadn't asked if he intended to accept.

'I'm afraid at the moment I can't tell you whether we'll be coming or not,' she answered politely. 'But I'll ask Sander to give you a ring.' Without further ado, she replaced the receiver, then sat staring blindly into space.

Even as a child Rhoda had been spoilt and spiteful. Surely this phone call was just spite, an attempt to cause trouble? Yet Rhoda had sounded so *sure* of her facts, and she had known Sander was out most evenings.

Feeling sick and agitated, Mia made an effort to brush the misgivings away. The fact that Jacqueline May was in London didn't mean a thing, she told herself sternly. And it wouldn't be hard for Rhoda to guess that, with Sander taking over the reins shortly, he would be working all hours.

But as soon as Mia picked up her book the doubts and uncertainties homed in once more, troublesome as a swarm of gnats. Suppose Rhoda was right and he was seeing Jacqueline May again? Assuring the glamorous model that having a wife was only a temporary inconvenience? Just waiting until he was the head of the bank, and Rhoda had married Philip, before he ended their marriage?

If he was, there was little she could do about it. Yet if he was, why had he suggested that they look for another house? Had that been merely a ploy to keep her quiet and out of his hair?

Making an effort, she tried again to dismiss everything Rhoda had said. It was being weak-minded in the extreme to let a vindictive woman unsettle her like this.

It was then that the tempting thought came. She could phone Sander's office. He'd given her his private number in case she needed to contact him, but she had never used it. When he answered she would know for certain that he wasn't at Bentham's with Jacqueline May.

She didn't have to speak, she could just replace the receiver as if it had been a wrongly dialled number, and he need never know she'd called. She felt ashamed of such subterfuge, but it would set the agonising doubts at rest.

On the other hand, she could phone him openly and ask how much longer he intended to stay. Tell him she was missing him... That at least was the truth.

Without further ado Mia picked up the phone.

She kept it ringing out for a long time, but there was no answer.

It seemed that Rhoda was right after all. His 'faithfulness' had lasted only as long as the honeymoon.

At eleven o'clock Mia went to bed, to toss and turn sleeplessly until, some time after midnight, she heard him return. She lay listening to the faint sound of the shower running, torn apart by jealousy and a misery too deep for tears.

He padded in, silent as some big cat and, without putting on the light, slipped into bed beside her.

Trying to breathe evenly, she lay quietly, feigning sleep. He was so close she could smell the freshness of shower gel, feel the warmth of his skin.

She jumped convulsively as his hand touched her breast.

'Something wrong?' he asked.

'You startled me,' she said raggedly. 'I was asleep.'

'You're lying through your teeth,' he informed her pleasantly. 'You were *pretending* to be asleep. So what's wrong?'

'Nothing's wrong,' she mumbled.

'Then why the play-acting?'

'I've got a headache.'

'That sounds like an excuse rather than an explanation. Suppose you tell me the simple truth?'

'Very well,' she snapped, 'the simple truth is I don't want you to touch me.'

Suddenly he was sitting up, leaning over her, and the light was on, shining down like a third degree.

Instinctively Mia jerked away, closing her eyes.

Sander took her chin in his hand, fingers spread against one cheek, thumb against the other, and turned her face to his. 'Look at me.'

For a brief moment she resisted his dominance. Then, knowing it was hopeless to try and hold out against him, she opened her eyes, blinking a little.

Softly he said, 'Now let's get one thing quite clear. Sex isn't mandatory. You have a perfect right to refuse, and I won't ever force you. But I won't allow any woman, not even my wife, to speak to me like that.'

'I . . . I . . .' Wishing she'd never embarked on this confrontation, she gulped miserably, and had to shut her eyes tightly to hold back betraying tears. Even so, one squeezed beneath her lid and trickled down her cheek.

Sander stopped its descent with the tip of his tongue, while his hand slid down to her breast. The lean fingers lightly brushing her nipple elicited an instant, uncontrollable response. Through the flimsy material of her nightdress, his lips closed over the taut tip, his tongue circling damply.

Mia made a little choked sound in her throat.

His hand began to stroke along the silken warmth of her inner thigh, and, unable to help herself, she put her arms around his neck and lifted her hips invitingly.

When he instantly drew away she gave a whimper of protest.

'Are you quite sure you want me to make love to you?' he asked.

'Yes ... Oh, yes!' she whispered.

Still he held back. 'So why did you pretend you didn't want me to touch you?'

She stiffened, and, the words wrenched from her, cried, 'Why did you pretend to be working until this time of night?'

'You sound as if you think I've come straight from someone else's bed to yours.'

'I don't think anything of the kind,' she denied, not altogether truthfully. 'I ... I just wondered where you'd been.'

'Why didn't you try asking me?'

Watching his mouth, with its impression of austerity so at variance with its warmly curved lower lip, Mia half shook her head. There were too many reasons, nearly all of them complicated.

'If you *had* asked me,' he went on, 'I would have told you that I've been taking a very important client out for a late meal. I haven't been making love to some other woman.'

Mia's doubts were dispelled by his words as morning mist was dispelled by the sun. He wouldn't lie to her. Only people who were weak or afraid needed to lie, and Sander was neither.

When she stayed silent, bemused by relief, he said with a kind of silky menace, 'Maybe I'd better prove it.'

He proved it to her complete satisfaction.

Afterwards, holding her in his arms, he said, 'I told you once before that one willing woman is all I need.'

Mia nestled closer. So long as *she* was that woman, even if he didn't love her, it was enough. Well, almost.

It was after dinner the following evening before she could bring herself to broach the subject of Rhoda's wedding.

When she did, Sander looked at her, a frown drawing his dark brows together. 'Do you want to go?'

'No!' Forcing herself to speak more moderately, she went on, 'I mean, not unless you do... And I'm sure Rhoda won't want me there.'

Slowly he said, 'Nevertheless I think we should go. It will look strange if we don't.' Ironically he added, 'We might even be able to lay a few ghosts.'

On Tuesday of the following week, Mia was about to set out to visit yet another house agent when Janet phoned to suggest that they had lunch together.

'Lovely,' Mia agreed enthusiastically.

'Shall we meet at Moonraker's? One o'clock?'

'I'll be there,' Mia promised.

Moonraker's was a wine-bar just off Oxford Street. Though unpretentious, it served some of the best and cheapest food in London.

Mia was waiting at a table for two when Janet breezed in.

The other girl examined her critically and exclaimed, 'You look fantastic! To bend the phrase a little, being a young man's darling certainly suits you.' Then seriously, '*Is* it working out?'

'Yes, it's working out fine.'

'I'm *delighted*,' Janet said, and meant it.

Then, finding it gave her a thrill to say the words, Mia remarked, 'Sander and I are looking for another house. Without much success so far, but it's quite exciting.'

'You can say that again!'

At Mia's raised brow, Janet crowed, 'Have I got things to tell you! But first let's order. I find love affects me strangely. Instead of going out and baying at the moon, I *eat*. No, I'm not pregnant,' she added with a grin. 'Though I hope to be as soon as Jon and I are married.'

Gratified by Mia's look of amazement, Janet launched into an account of Jon's whirlwind courtship.

'I know it sounds hackneyed, but for both of us it was love at first sight. He said, "I've only been waiting for the right woman and now I've found her, so why wait any longer?" And I felt the same. Except, of course, I'd been waiting for the right man...' Excitement making her barely coherent, Janet babbled on happily.

As they tucked into a *paella a la valenciana* and sipped glasses of chilled white wine, Mia asked, 'So do I take it the wedding's imminent?'

'It is,' Janet told her smugly. 'Thanks to you. A well-aimed bouquet can work wonders! When I caught yours, Jon said, "That makes you our next bride. I like to keep up these old traditions, so as soon as you get to know me better I'll go down on my knees and propose in style." I thought at the time he was joking, but he did!

'What do you think of that?' She waved her left hand, making the hoop of diamonds on her third finger sparkle.

'It's gorgeous.' Mia gave her admiration unstintingly. 'So when's the great day?'

'June the thirtieth. I hope you'll be my matron of honour, though it's only at the local register office.'

'Try stopping me!'

'We're house-hunting like mad,' Janet went on cheerfully. 'Jon's just been promoted and had a very nice increase in salary, so we're trying to buy a place with a small garden for when Junior comes along. We're hoping for something not too far out so Jon won't have to spend hours every day commuting.'

Forking in the last of her rice, she added, 'I mustn't be too long, I've got a desk full of work. To tell you the truth, I won't be sorry when I can leave. It's not the same without you. And since your wedding, Philip has scarcely been civil. It's almost as if he blames *me* in some way...

'Being a prospective father certainly doesn't suit him; he's as miserable as sin... Oh, *blast* my unruly tongue! The last thing I wanted to do was worry you.'

'It's quite all right,' Mia assured her steadily. 'You haven't.'

She spoke the truth. The knowledge that Philip was miserable made her feel sorry for him, despite his deceit, but it didn't wrench her heart as once it would have done.

'Well, I must dash,' Janet said briskly. 'It's been lovely seeing you. I'm so *glad* everything's working out well. Aren't we a fortunate pair?'

She put the money for half the bill on the table and fastened her bag. 'I'll be in touch in a day or two. Carry on with the house-hunting, and don't forget to let me know if you get lucky.'

When the girl had gone, Mia ordered a coffee and drank it slowly. She had answered Janet's question about her marriage with more confidence than she actually felt.

Physically it was all and more than she could ever have hoped for. The nights spent in Sander's arms were the most wonderful she had ever known. But while she was fairly sure he no longer despised her, that was as far as she could go. She had no real idea what, if anything, he felt for her.

On the other hand, her emotions were dangerously simple. She was happy when she was with him, lost when they were apart. She loved him with a depth of feeling that swamped all else, and longed for his love with a desire that constantly stung her heart.

In his deep, attractive voice he whispered that she was beautiful, warm and sweet and enchantingly sexy. That he wanted her more than he'd ever wanted any woman. But, even when his dark head lay heavy on her breast in the aftermath of passion, he never so much as breathed the word love.

Nor had he ever asked again if she loved him.

Towards teatime, after several hours of intensive house-hunting, Mia came out of Ashleigh Adams with a sigh. There was no lack of houses and flats, even the odd castle, but nothing she had been shown so far was remotely what they wanted.

On foot, because although the sky was overcast it was still fine, Mia went to visit the penultimate house agent on her list. There she was offered what sounded like the house of her dreams.

Tall Trees, an old manor house with a couple of acres of wooded garden, would, unless sold privately, be going on to the open market in a week or so's time, Douglas Wentworth told her.

A careful, precise man, he described it as, 'An excellent family house. Spacious, without being over-large, and both practical and picturesque.'

He showed her a picture of a low, rambling place, stone-built and mellow, with a sunny terrace leading to sloping lawns. He added, 'Full details and a complete set of photographs will be to hand within the next few days.'

Though set in pleasant countryside close to a pretty village, Tall Trees was within easy commuting distance of town. This was reflected in the asking price, which was astronomical. But Sander had left the question of price open, saying merely that if they saw something they liked they could consider whether or not it was worth it.

When Mia gave him her name, evidently recognising it, Mr Wentworth said with additional respect, 'I'll let you know as soon as the keys are available. I'm sure that you and Mr Davison will find it ideal.'

Thrilled to bits, Mia walked back to Crombie Square with wings on her heels. It was just after six o'clock when she arrived home, and she wasn't expecting Sander until eight. Feeling she must share the good news straight away or burst with excitement, she rang Janet's flat.

A familiar voice answered, 'Fifi's massage parlour.'

'Fool!' Mia said, adding, 'I wondered if you'd be home.'

'Just got in,' Janet told her cheerfully. 'So what's new?'

Mia poured it all out, ending, 'Though I've no idea if we can afford it.'

'I shouldn't worry about that,' Janet told her drily.

'It looks such a *lovely* old place,' Mia enthused. 'Oh, I do hope Sander likes it!'

A smile in her voice, Janet observed, 'Loving you as much as he does, I'm sure he'll be happy living anywhere you——'

'Do you really think he loves me?' Mia broke in, the eager question popping out before she could prevent it.

Janet sounded surprised. 'Well, of course . . . What other reason could he have had for rushing you off your feet the way he did?'

As Mia hesitated, wondering what to say, the other girl went on, 'Surely he's told you how he feels about you?'

'Not really,' Mia mumbled.

'Have you told him how you feel about him?'

'Not really,' Mia repeated.

'Well, it's fairly obvious that you're fathoms deep in love with him,' Janet said. Then, consideringly, 'But men can be very blind. I expect he feels insecure and jealous.'

At Mia's startled silence, Janet added, 'Of Philip, I mean. At the wedding Sander looked as if he could cheerfully have killed him! I expect that like most strong men he hates to feel vulnerable, and loving someone makes you vulnerable, especially if you're not sure how they feel . . .

'But to get back to the house. When you tell Sander about it, just make sure he knows how much you want it, and I'll take a bet that it'll be yours. I'm convinced he'd give you the moon and stars if they were his to give.'

Mia put down the phone, her heart light. If Sander loved her, and Janet clearly thought he did, the moon and stars were already hers.

After some reflection, Mia decided to wait until she had the full details before telling Sander about Tall Trees. So during dinner that evening when he asked if she'd made any progress, hiding her excitement as best she could, she said vaguely, 'Wentworth's told me that there might be just what we're looking for coming on to the market quite soon.'

Then, to change the subject, she went on to tell him Janet's news.

'I already know.' He grinned at her complacently. 'Jon told me. He's been walking on air for days now.'

Casually, Mia remarked, 'Janet told me he'd been promoted.'

'Don't think I'm being kind to him.' Sander read her thoughts with his usual accuracy. 'He's earned it. I just brought it forward a month or two.'

'I think that's kind,' she said firmly, and was amused to see that, briefly, he looked almost embarrassed.

Next morning, after Sander had given her a wake-up kiss that turned first into a romp, then into something just as strenuous but quieter and much more intimate, they lay entwined for a while, relaxed and contented.

His long fingers absentmindedly stroking the side of her neck, he remarked, 'I'm sorry to have neglected you so much lately.'

With a delicious little chuckle, Mia confessed, 'I don't *feel* neglected.'

Sander bit her ear and said sternly, 'Less of the levity while your lord and master is endeavouring to apologise.'

'There's nothing to apologise for,' she assured him. 'All the same, I'll be glad when you don't need to work quite such long hours and we've got more time together.'

'So will I.'

His answer made happiness blossom inside her like a flower. Maybe one day soon he would tell her he loved her... If Janet was right, he might only be waiting for her to admit it was him she cared for, not Philip.

Dared she do that? she wondered, remembering his 'third objective'. But she had long since realised that her first assessment of the situation had been an erroneous one. She had told herself that, so long as he wasn't aware of her love, she would be safe. That he could only hurt her if he knew.

But of course that wasn't so. The mere fact that she loved him, whether he knew it or not, left her wide open to being hurt. It was simply a matter of trusting him not to crucify her deliberately.

Her other fear had been that if he knew he'd won, if she ceased to be a challenge, he'd tire of her sooner. But, although she would have been hard put to it to say why, that fear had receded into the background until it no longer worried her.

Brushing her lips against the smooth tanned skin of his shoulder, she began, 'Sander, I . . .'

He stopped her words with a kiss, then said with evident regret, 'There's nothing I'd like better than to stay here and make love to you all day, but I've got a meeting with the board in a little over an hour.'

Throwing back the duvet, he got out of bed and headed naked for the bathroom, his smoothly muscled body magnificently male.

Mia sighed. Oh, well, she'd tell him as soon as the time was right.

While he was showering, she washed her face and hands, pulled on her white silky robe and went down to the kitchen. Having switched on the radio, she sang along with it as she squeezed oranges, fed slices of wholemeal bread into the toaster, and made a pot of coffee.

Dressed in a grey pinstriped business suit, Sander took his usual place at the breakfast bar and, lean fingers stroking over his freshly shaven jaw, remarked, 'You sound happy.'

'That's because I am happy,' she informed him blithely.

'It's obvious that making love in the morning suits you. We'll have to make a habit of it.' Though his smile was teasing, his expression grew curiously soft as he watched her cheeks turn pink.

When, some thirty minutes later, he was about to leave the house, he tilted her chin with his usual proprietorial gesture. His eyes lingering on her shiny face with its neat nose and generous mouth, the winged brows and beautiful, long-lashed eyes, he said, 'You're one of the few women I've ever known who look even sexier without make-up.' But his kiss seemed to hold a warmth, a tenderness, that had less to do with sex than with affection.

Mia held on to this thought, basking in the sunshine it created.

While she was clearing away the breakfast dishes, the phone rang. Picking up the extension, she said a cheerful, 'Hello?'

'Mia darling, it's me——'

'Philip!' It was a horrified exclamation. 'You must be out of your mind, ringing here!'

'Don't hang up on me!' The urgency of Philip's plea momentarily stayed her hand. 'I've got to talk to you and I've only——'

'I don't want to talk to you. There's absolutely nothing left to say.' She dropped the receiver back on its cradle as if it were red-hot, more shaken than she cared to admit. The very last thing she wanted was him calling here, causing trouble when things might just be starting to work out.

CHAPTER NINE

FOR the rest of the day Mia was on tenterhooks every time the phone rang. But when the evening came and went and there had been no further calls from Philip, she began to relax a little.

That night Sander was very late, and Mia was asleep before he got home. He didn't disturb her, and when she stirred and opened her eyes it was morning, and he was already up and in the shower.

She felt a sudden intense disappointment. She'd wanted to wake, as she had so many times now, to find Sander propped on one elbow watching her. Waiting for her. Sometimes he refused to wait and wakened her with a kiss or a caress from those long, seductive fingers.

Of course, she could join him in the shower.

A glance at the bedside clock showed her that he hadn't a lot of time, and she didn't want him to have to rush his breakfast. Lately, she thought, though he was superbly fit, he had looked a shade tired, as if the strain of working such long hours was beginning to tell.

When he appeared in the kitchen, handsome and vital and sexy as hell, and moved her silky blonde hair aside to drop a kiss on her nape, she wished she'd followed her first impulse.

As they ate breakfast, Sander glanced up and said, 'By the way, I forgot to tell you that we're going out tonight. Jon was given four tickets for that new show everyone's raving about. He asked if we'd like to join

Janet and himself, and I accepted for both of us. I hope you don't mind?'

'Of course not.' Mia's eyes sparkled. 'A night out will be lovely.'

They were just finishing their coffee when Mrs Rose brought up the morning post. Sander glanced through it and, having passed Mia a letter addressed to her, began to open his own.

She looked at the neat, intricate writing that was only too familiar and felt sick.

As she stared at the envelope as if it was a rattle-snake, Sander asked lightly, 'What's the matter, scared it might be a bill?'

Her impulse was to tear it up without further ado, but if she did he was sure to wonder why. Forcing a smile, she opened it.

Mia darling,

I can't go on like this any longer. Every day seems so empty. I've *got* to talk to you. Meet me some-where, anywhere you say, only please make it soon. I can't believe you've stopped loving me and I...

Hands shaking, she thrust the letter back into the envelope without reading any more. When she glanced up, Sander was watching her, his eyes thoughtful.

'You look upset,' he remarked. 'Is there something wrong?'

'No, no...it's nothing,' she lied.

His jaw seemed to tighten as though he'd clenched his teeth, but to her great relief he said no more.

When he was leaving he kissed her as usual, but this time his kiss held no warmth, only an almost fierce possessiveness.

As soon as he'd gone, Mia screwed up the envelope and its contents and threw it on to the fire. But the harm had been done, she admitted bleakly. Sander was no fool, he knew she'd lied about the letter, and had, almost certainly, guessed why.

The knowledge made her skin grow heated and her heart grow chilled.

Oh, damn Philip, she thought helplessly. Then honesty made her admit that she had only herself to blame. Sander had given her the opportunity to tell him the truth and she hadn't taken it.

She had been afraid. Afraid that his anger would be directed against her. Afraid that he wouldn't believe she hadn't encouraged Philip in some way. Afraid also, after his threat in the gazebo, of what he might do to Philip.

But she couldn't, *wouldn't* let this come between them, she vowed. As soon as Sander got home, she'd tell him the truth and chance the consequences.

In the event she had no opportunity to talk to him. He arrived home with barely enough time to shower and change before they had to set off for the theatre.

After the show, which proved to be both lively and funny, they went on to Magnum's for a late meal, and didn't start home until well after midnight.

During the evening Sander had appeared to be his usual self, joining in the talk and laughter, but as soon as they were alone he lapsed into a brooding silence.

Perhaps when they were in bed she could talk to him, Mia thought. But for the first time since their wedding night he turned his back on her.

Feeling utterly desolate, she stared at his broad, muscular shoulders, and tried to pluck up sufficient nerve to begin, but he looked so unapproachable that strands of mingled regret and misery tied her tongue.

Next morning, as though the whole thing had stayed at the forefront of her mind, Mia awoke to immediate remembrance and a set determination to try to clear the air. She turned to Sander, to find him lying quietly, watching her, but this time his green eyes were cool, his face stern.

Swallowing, she said, 'There's something I want to tell you.'

'A confession?' he asked, his voice hard yet brittle as glass.

'Sort of,' she admitted, flushing a little. 'It's about...about Philip.'

Sander's expression grew even more austere. 'I already know you're playing around with him again behind my back.'

'I'm doing no such thing,' she denied vehemently.

Just for a moment Sander looked shaken, then he asked curtly, 'How many times have you met Measham in secret?'

'I haven't set eyes on him since our wedding-day.' The simple words had the ring of truth, but it was impossible to tell whether he believed her or not.

Sitting up, he leaned over her, his brilliant gaze searching her face. 'Don't try to deny you've been in touch. That letter was from him.'

'Yes, it was. I'm sorry, I should have told you straight away. But it threw me. I was scared——'

'I bet you were!' Sander interrupted tersely. 'Just how often has he written? How many times has he phoned you?'

'Only once. He rang the day before yesterday, but I told him I didn't want to speak to him, and I burnt his letter without even reading it.' She gazed up at him, her grey eyes wide and pleading.

Sander's lip curled. 'It's no use playing "look how innocent I am". Rhoda warned me what was going on.'

'There's nothing going on,' Mia choked. 'Rhoda's just out to make trouble.' But, even as she spoke, she wished she'd kept silent. The last time she'd said those words Sander had accused *her* of being the troublemaker.

Contempt in his voice, he demanded, 'Do you call trying to keep the man who's the father of her child making trouble?'

It was no use, Mia thought hopelessly. Perhaps if she'd told him about the phone call Rhoda had made to her... But she hadn't.

Taking a deep breath, she assured him, 'I haven't encouraged Philip in any way. I just want him to leave me alone, and that's the truth, believe me.'

'I wish I could.' Sander's heavily lashed eyes were sombre.

Before Mia could make any further attempt to convince him, he leapt out of bed and headed for the bathroom.

Showered and dressed, he refused breakfast because of the lateness of the hour, and, after swallowing a cup of coffee, was about to leave for the bank when the phone shrilled.

Reaching out a long arm, he picked up the receiver, only to replace it almost immediately.

'A wrong number?' Mia asked, her heart in her mouth.

'Either that, or whoever's on the other end didn't expect me to be still at home.'

Sander's tone was cutting, and before Mia could catch her breath he was gone, the door slamming behind him.

Had the caller been Philip? Clearly Sander suspected as much. She sighed heavily. He'd left without giving her his usual kiss, or confirming their lunch date.

She had to go into town to keep a dental appointment and, a couple of days previously, Sander had arranged to meet her afterwards.

Just before she was ready to leave the house the phone rang again. She paused before answering, worried in case it might be Philip.

When she forced herself to lift the receiver, Sander's voice said brusquely, 'I'm afraid I can't make lunch. Something's come up that I have to deal with personally.'

'Oh.' Biting on her disappointment, she asked forlornly, 'Are you working late tonight?'

'I don't expect to be.'

With that she had to be content.

After keeping her twelve o'clock appointment, Mia found herself at a loose end. Sander had been going to take her to eat at Greasham's. Now she wondered where to head for. She didn't feel comfortable going to the Park Lane restaurant by herself.

It was a day of sunshine and showers, and, as she stood hesitating, large spots of rain began to spatter on to the pavement.

All at once she thought of Cedric's, a small basement restaurant Sander had taken her to the previous week. It was a quiet, modest place where the food was good and the atmosphere quiet and friendly. Best of all, it was just round the corner.

Seated at one of the little side tables, Mia ordered pizza and salad and a glass of Fleurie, and listened to a tape of guitar music being played softly. When her food arrived she spread a napkin on her knee, and had just raised her wine glass to her lips when she glanced up—and froze.

Sitting at a table on the far side of the room was Sander, and, opposite him, Jacqueline May, dressed dramatically in black and white. Her skin looked very pale against her scarlet lip-gloss, and her frizzy hair was dark and vital, held in place by a twisted rope of black and white fabric which encircled her forehead.

The two were in profile, and it was immediately obvious to Mia that this was no business lunch. They were both leaning forward to talk intimately, confidentially, and at one point, when the model's face showed naked emotion, Sander reached across the snowy cloth and took the slim, restless hand, holding it in both of his.

So Rhoda had been right after all. Mia sat quite still, transfixed, as if mortally wounded. She'd believed him when he'd said one woman was all he needed. Now she stared at the pair and felt as if her very life blood were draining away.

Afraid that the fixity of her gaze might draw their attention and make Sander look her way, she compelled herself to concentrate on her food, but her throat had closed up tight and she couldn't swallow. Somehow she forced a mouthful down, and almost gagged as her stomach revolted.

She wanted desperately to jump to her feet and run, but pride kept her in her seat. If she stood up to go, Sander might notice her, and she couldn't bear it if he saw her and realised how shattered she was.

The pair had reached the coffee stage when she'd first looked across, and now she saw that Sander was paying the bill. As they walked towards the door she ducked her head in the hope that he wouldn't spot her.

He didn't. Wrapped up in his tall, willowy companion, he went past without so much as a glance.

Leaving the meal untouched, Mia paid her bill and, having assured the anxious waiter than everything was fine, she just wasn't hungry, fled. She felt sick and giddy, like someone who had been on a merry-go-round too long.

Scarcely noticing the showers, which soon turned to heavy, continuous rain, she walked the streets, trying desperately to rid herself of the picture of those two dark heads so close together. But each time she hurled it away it returned, boomerang-like, to hit her even harder.

Eventually, wet to the skin and tired out, she found herself back at Crombie Square. When she'd taken off her saturated clothes and towelled her hair, she prepared an evening meal and waited, taut and miserable, for Sander to come home.

It was almost eight o'clock before she heard his key in the lock. He merely glanced into the living-room before going upstairs to get changed.

Staring after him, Mia thought that perhaps if she just tried to act normally he would tell her. Tell her what? 'I said I couldn't make lunch, then I took my mistress out'?

While Sander ate, she pushed her food round her plate, taking an occasional sip of wine. Suddenly realising she'd been abnormally quiet, she was trying to marshal her thoughts and find something to say when he asked carelessly, 'How did you get on at the dentist's?'

'The check-up was fine, I don't need anything doing. Mr Marshall said...' Finding she was going into unnecessary detail, babbling, she pulled herself up short.

'So what did you do about lunch?' Sander wanted to know. 'Did you eat in town?'

'Yes, I...'

His gaze met, and held her reluctant glance. 'Where did you go?'

Startled by the sharp question, she stammered, 'I . . . I don't remember the name of the place.'

He gave her a glinting look from beneath thick, dark lashes. 'Could it have been Cedric's?'

Her heart lurched. 'You saw me!' she accused.

'Yes, I saw you.' His voice was brusque. 'Why try to hide the fact that you'd seen me?'

'I . . . I didn't want you to think that I was——'

'Spying on me? And were you?'

'Of course not,' she denied, white-lipped. 'I just went in there by chance.'

'So why didn't you ask for an explanation?'

'I didn't feel I had the right,' she said with difficulty.

'Yes, it would have smacked of the pot calling the kettle black.'

Biting back the futile anger, she begged, 'Please, Sander, I don't want to quarrel——'

'What a docile little wife!' he mocked.

His ridicule was like the dropping of a lighted match into a pool of petrol. She jumped to her feet, pushing back her chair. But, before she could run, he reached out a long arm and caught her wrist.

'Let go of me!' she cried furiously, trying to slap his hand away.

'Temper,' he chided.

'Oh, go to hell!' she choked. 'I just hope the next time you have lunch with your mistress she poisons you!'

Sander laughed as if genuinely amused. 'I'd quite forgotten you could be so fiery. But I fail to see what all the fuss is in aid of. You love another man, so you can't be jealous... And in case Measham doesn't come up to scratch, I promise I won't neglect you in bed.'

He was treating the whole thing as if it was some kind of game, when it had caused her so much heartache.

'You said you only needed one willing woman.' Mia threw his earlier words back at him.

'That's true.' He sounded unconcerned. 'But I didn't say I couldn't cope with two.'

'You haven't got two.'

'Don't you think Jacqueline...?'

'Oh, I'm sure *she's* willing enough...' Mia bit her lip hard. Oh, dear God, she was acting just like a fishwife, but anger and misery between them made a cruel goad. 'I mean that while you're seeing her I won't sleep with you.'

'Do you think you'll be able to hold out when I start making love to you?'

Trying not to allow emotion to swallow her up, she said raggedly, 'Yes, I do. I...'

'Come to bed with me now and prove it.'

'I don't... I won't...'

Ignoring her splutterings, he swept her up into his arms and carried her into the bedroom. There, despite her struggles, he stripped her.

Half sobbing, she cried, 'Leave me alone! I hate you! Go back to *her*. I won't just be made use of whenever it suits you!'

'You'll do exactly what I want you to do,' he grated.

Still fully dressed, he held her down while, his mouth at her breast, he used his long fingers to devastating effect.

When she was reduced to a quivering mass of sensations, balanced on the brink of ecstasy, he pulled off his own clothes and with his first thrust sent her tumbling over the edge. Nails biting into his back, she moaned and shuddered against him, while with a skill that amounted almost to cruelty he kept her spiralling downwards.

Afterwards, eyes closed, she lay still and spent, his powerful body still dominating hers. He brushed a strand of silky ash-blonde hair back from her cheek and said with soft violence, 'Make no mistake about it. While you're still my wife I shall take you whenever I want you.'

'You said you would never force me, that I had every right to say no,' she whispered painfully.

Lifting himself away, Sander turned on his back. 'That was before I knew about Measham.'

Bitterly she demanded, 'What was it you said about the pot calling the kettle black?'

At nine o'clock the following morning, Mr Wentworth rang to say that the keys to Tall Trees would be available by the end of the following week. He said, 'The particulars are to hand now, if you'd like me to send them on.'

Mia thanked him and said that to save the trouble of posting them she would call in later that day and pick them up. She went with a heavy heart, all her earlier excitement and optimism gone.

The details and the photographs only served to confirm that Tall Trees was everything she had hoped for, and more. But, the situation being what it was, Sander was hardly likely to be interested in buying a house. If he ever had been.

That evening, when they'd eaten an almost silent meal, after a great deal of hesitation she gave him the folder.

He looked through it without making any comment.

When she couldn't bear the suspense a moment longer, she asked, 'What do you think?'

'What do *you* think?' Without giving anything away, he returned the ball to her court.

Staring down at her hands, Mia spoke the exact truth. 'I think it's lovely. The kind of house I've always dreamt of living in.'

'Yes, it seems a beautiful old place.' His comment lifted her spirits until he added, 'But in the circumstances I can't see that we need another house.'

Her face pale and strained, but schooled into some semblance of composure, she braced herself to hear the worst and asked, 'Are you intending to end our marriage?'

Sander looked at her, his eyes cold as the Arctic Ocean. 'Aren't you the one who's thinking of doing that?'

'You mean because of Jacqueline May?'

'I mean because of Measham. You are planning to run away with him, aren't you?'

'Run away with him?' Mia echoed. Then, anger overriding everything else, she cried, 'Divorce me if you want to—I won't lift a finger to stop you. But you needn't try to put the blame on me. No matter what Rhoda's told you, I am *not* planning to run away with Philip...'

Sander's face seemed carved out of stone. She could have been talking to a statue, Mia thought with despair.

'Please *listen* to me...' she begged.

But there seemed to be no way she could reach him. It was as if they were on opposite sides of an abyss with no bridge between them.

Passionately, she cried, 'Oh, God, what's the use? If you really believe I'm the kind of unfeeling bitch who'd try to take another woman's man, a woman who's *pregnant*, then even if Jacqueline May didn't exist there's no hope for our marriage!'

The rush of adrenalin made her feel giddy, and the blood pounded in her ears. Whirling, she ran from the house, down the steps and out into the cold, heavy drizzle of the May night.

Seeing a passer-by give her a curious look from beneath his black umbrella, she slowed her wild flight to a walk, and stumbled blindly on, sobbing under her breath.

Before she'd gone more than a few yards she was wet through and chilled to the bone, her blouse plastered to her, her thin skirt clinging damply to her knees at every step. But nothing on earth would induce her to go back, she thought wildly. Not that Sander would want her back. He would probably decide he was well rid of her.

As she turned out of Crombie Square, a taxi slowed, as if the driver, catching sight of her, half expected her to hail him. But she had no money. And where could she go? Not to her father's...

Then, like a benediction, she thought of Janet. Janet would lend her the cab fare and give her a bed for the night without asking a lot of questions.

Just as Mia lifted her hand, she became aware of footsteps rounding the corner. A swift glance showed her Sander, his face a bleak mask of anger, striding purposefully towards her.

She dived into the taxi and, slamming the door, said hurriedly, 'I want to go to number twenty-seven Elmslea Gardens, Marylebone.'

The vehicle was on the point of pulling away when the door was wrenched open, and Mia was hauled out unceremoniously.

With a curse the startled driver applied his brakes. 'What the devil's going on?'

'Just a domestic tiff,' Sander said smoothly.

A middle-aged man clearly concerned for his would-be passenger, the cabby eyed them uncertainly.

Keeping a firm grip on Mia's arm, Sander added, 'This is my wife.' Then, impatiently, 'Ask her if you don't believe me.'

Obviously a devotee of old Hollywood movies, the driver demanded, 'Well, lady, is this guy your husband?'

Just for a moment Mia played with the notion of swearing she'd never seen Sander before, then, her nerve failing her, she admitted, 'Yes, he is. But I still want to go to Elmslea——'

'You're going nowhere,' Sander interrupted. Holding her securely, he extracted a five-pound note from his wallet and tossed it into the cab.

A shade apologetically the driver said, 'Sorry, lady, I make it a rule never to get mixed up in domestic rows,' and, before Mia could make any further plea, the taxi was drawing away.

Struggling to pull her arm from Sander's grip, she cried, 'Let me go! You have no right to——'

'As your husband I have every right. Now stop acting like an hysterical child and put this on.'

She found herself bundled into Sander's light mac and marched back the way she'd come.

Once they were inside, she tore herself free. Defying his anger, she faced him, her pale face shiny with the rain, her hair a darkened straggle of rats'-tails, the raincoat swamping her, its sleeves coming over her hands. 'You can't *make* me stay with you!'

He too was dishevelled, raindrops on his dark hair, the shoulders of his blue shirt wet, his tie awry. Looking suddenly weary, he said, 'That's true. But a short time ago you swore you weren't thinking of running away with Measham.'

'Nor am I.'

'Then why are you so determined to go?'

'I thought I'd made that clear,' she said stiffly. 'I don't intend to stay with a man who flaunts his mistress, a man who thinks I'm nothing but a heartless bitch.' Her voice broke and bitter tears welled up and ran down her cheeks. Fiercely she wiped them away. 'I *won't* stay!'

Gently he asked, 'Would it make any difference if I told you I don't think you're either heartless or a bitch? If I told you that yesterday was the first time I've seen Jacqueline since before we were married?'

Wanting to believe him, she whispered, 'But why did you let me think . . . ?'

'Why did you jump to conclusions?'

'Because Rhoda said . . .'

When Mia came to an abrupt stop, Sander demanded sharply, 'What did Rhoda say?'

'Oh, what's the use? I doubt if you'd believe me if I told you.'

'Try me.' He sounded stern.

Mia repeated the telephone conversation as near word for word as possible, in a voice that was deliberately flat, devoid of emotion.

'So that's why you acted so out of character when I got home that night!' After studying her face for a moment, he added wryly, 'So which of us do you believe, Rhoda or me?'

Mia's softly rounded chin came up. 'I might ask you the same.'

Obliquely he answered, 'Mother never did like Rhoda. She always said my cousin was untruthful and vindictive.' Briskly he added, 'It's about time you got out of those wet things.'

'Sander . . .' she had to be sure ' . . . do you *want* me to stay?'

A muscle jerked in his jaw as though he'd set his teeth, but, apart from that one small betraying movement, his dark face was unreadable. 'Yes, I want you to stay.'

'Why?'

'Why do you think?'

Her sudden glow of hope faded. Fool, she berated herself silently. She knew quite well why he wanted her to stay. The actual handing over of power at the bank wasn't yet complete, and until that had taken place he'd need her by his side for the look of the thing.

'Because of your father's will,' she said dully.

A strange look flickered across his face, but was gone before she could make any attempt to analyse it.

'That's not the only reason.' Roughly he gathered her up, raincoat and all, and kissed her mouth with a savage hunger. 'I want you. I want you in my life, in my home, in my bed.'

Later that night, when the euphoria of Sander's lovemaking had faded and, his breathing light and even, he slept by her side, Mia lay wide awake, feeling curiously cold and alone.

On the surface things had been smoothed over, but underneath, lurking like sharks, there were still doubts and uncertainties.

Thinking over what had taken place, she realised that Sander had never actually *denied* anything. All he'd said was, 'Would it make any difference if I told you...?' He hadn't explained *why* he'd been lunching with his ex-girlfriend when he'd let *her* down. Nor had he condemned Rhoda, merely cited what his mother had thought of her.

One thing—perhaps the only thing—Mia was certain of was that he still wanted her. Half a loaf, she thought—and, like someone starving, found that even a small crust was better than no bread at all.

Over the next few days, endeavouring not to think about Jacqueline May, Mia did her best to ignore all the misgivings and carry on as if everything in the garden was lovely.

Each night as she and Sander lay together, physically as close as two people could be, she prayed that he might come to care a little. But passion was the only emotion he displayed. Perhaps the only emotion he felt. She had no way of knowing. Always he withdrew behind mental barriers that kept her out. Though she lay in his arms, she was unable to reach him. Though they talked, she was unable to communicate.

Another inescapable worry was that Philip was making every effort to contact her. Recognising his writing, she tore up several hand-delivered notes without reading them, and each time she heard his voice she slammed the phone down.

Disturbed and distracted by such unexpected tenacity, she wondered whether to tell Sander, then decided against it. He was looking tired and drawn. The actual take-over of power at the bank was only a few days away and, working even harder on the last-minute details, he had more than enough on his mind. Surely, if she kept on ignoring all Philip's attempts to reach her, he'd give up?

The thing that really puzzled her was *why* he was being so persistent. It wasn't like him. He'd always hated emotional upsets and avoided confrontations whenever possible.

For his part, Sander neither mentioned Philip's name nor asked Mia any questions, but on the rare occasions he was home he watched her constantly.

Feeling harassed and guilty, all she could do was pray that he hadn't guessed what was going on.

Since that last traumatic scene he had said nothing about the house, and it came as a glad surprise when on the Thursday morning, as he was leaving for the office, he brought up the subject by asking coolly, 'Are you still interested in seeing Tall Trees?'

'Yes, I am. Very interested.' She made no attempt to hide her enthusiasm.

A look that could have been relief flashed in his green eyes, but was swiftly masked, as he added casually, 'Then I suggest we take a look this weekend and, if we like it, go ahead with the purchase.'

'Oh, *yes*!' Mia was oddly, irrationally convinced that if they lived in a lovely old house like that, a happy family house, everything would come right. Throwing her arms around his neck, she exclaimed joyfully, 'That sounds wonderful. I can hardly wait!'

For a moment or two the barriers came down, and she could have sworn Sander's emotion matched hers as he crushed her close, his cheek against her hair. Then with a brief, hard kiss he was gone.

Her heart singing, she almost danced into the kitchen. If he was considering buying the house, surely he must be expecting their marriage to last, must care for her just a tiny bit? Perhaps when he got home tonight . . .

She spent most of the day weaving hopes and fantasies into a shining dream for the future.

CHAPTER TEN

THE handing-over of power completed at last, that evening the executives of Davison Lazenby were giving a party in Sander's honour.

Wanting him to be proud of her, Mia put on the most elegant of her dresses, a simple white silk sheath that relied on the cut and the beauty of the material for its stunning effect. The only jewellery she wore, apart from her engagement ring, was the collar of pearls Sander had given her on their wedding-day.

She was ready and waiting, her make-up carefully applied, her ash-blonde hair taken up in a smooth chignon, when he got home. Having hoped for so much she was bitterly disappointed when, after gazing at her for what seemed an age, he neither spoke nor kissed her.

Though his expression was enigmatic, giving nothing away, she knew with certainty that since he'd left her something bad had happened and the barriers were up again with a vengeance.

The party, held at the sumptuous suite the bank kept for its entertaining, was a small but glittering affair. Just the bank's executives and their wives or lady friends had been invited. Nearly all the women were elaborately gowned, and Mia was glad she'd worn the most striking thing in her wardrobe.

As Sander's wife she was the cynosure of all eyes, the women's mainly envious, the men's both admiring and respectful.

166

Along with their impeccable evening clothes, most of the men wore an almost visible aura of wealth and power. Yet each treated Sander with marked deference. He moved amongst them, suave and smiling, effortlessly in control, but Mia was aware of strain and tension beneath the relaxed image he projected.

She was standing between Jon and Janet and looking across the room to where Sander was deep in conversation with one of his silver-haired colleagues, when Jon commented shrewdly, 'Sander seems a bit uptight tonight.'

'I think he's been working too hard,' Mia excused.

'I expect you're right,' Janet agreed, adding, 'With him putting in such long hours it must have been pretty lonely for you. I bet you're jolly glad that control of the bank is finally in his hands and he can be at home more.'

'In some respects it's a pity you didn't delay getting married until after he'd taken over the reins,' Jon remarked. 'You might have managed a longer honeymoon, and you wouldn't have started your married life by being alone so much.'

'But surely he had to be married *before* he could take control?' Mia objected.

'Whatever gave you that idea?' Jon sounded surprised.

'Sander said he . . .' Mia stopped, then floundered on, 'I thought that under the terms of his father's will he had to be married first.'

'That's not what he told me,' Jon answered decidedly. 'As I understand it, the old man didn't approve of these modern "relationships" and hoped to see his son married. But it was a wish, not a stipulation. I should imagine he knew Sander too well to attempt to impose conditions.'

Mia stood quite still, her thoughts whirling like a blizzard of snowflakes. It didn't make sense. Could Jon be wrong? No, surely not; the two men had been close friends for years.

For the rest of the evening, though Mia made an effort to smile and talk and mingle with the other guests, part of her mind was on what Jon had told her. As soon as she and Sander were alone, she decided, she would ask him for the truth.

But fate was against her. The party dragged on, and they didn't get back to Crombie Square until very late. Then, as though Sander knew her intention and intended to thwart it, he stayed downstairs to have a nightcap.

Mia went to bed, tired out but determined to remain awake until he joined her. The next thing she knew it was morning and he had already left for the bank.

By the time she had showered and dressed it was gone ten o'clock, so after she had made herself some toast and coffee she went to see Douglas Wentworth. The keys to Tall Trees in her possession, she spent the rest of the day in a dither of impatience waiting for Sander to come home.

She was preparing a special dinner when he phoned to say he would be late. She had hoped that now the handing over of authority was completed he would be home at a more normal time. Swallowing her disappointment as best she could, she asked, 'How late? Will you want a meal when you get in?'

'No, I'll be eating out.' He sounded cool to the point of curtness.

The question, who with? hung on the tip of her tongue, but somehow she managed to bite it back. If he was taking Jacqueline May to dinner she didn't want to know. Liar! Of course she wanted to know. But he was hardly likely to admit it.

Putting the steak back in the fridge, she cooked herself a plain omelette, but once it was in front of her she found her appetite had vanished.

She did her best to immerse herself in a new paperback, but it was impossible to concentrate. Superimposed on the print were images of Sander's strong hand taking Jacqueline May's slim, restless one, of two clear-cut faces intent on each other, two dark heads close together.

It was after eleven when Sander got back. Wanting to jump up and go to him, to ask him where he'd been, Mia forced herself to sit still. Act casual, she adjured herself, not like a jealously suspicious wife.

Walking over to the sideboard, he queried, 'Do you want anything?' When she shook her head he poured himself a stiff whisky and tossed it back, before disappearing upstairs.

Though in many ways tough and formidable, he was usually even-tempered and easy to live with. The kind of man who would instigate a morning or evening romp, and whistle while he shaved. Tonight he was quiet and remote, as gloomy as she had ever seen him.

Trying to behave as if nothing was amiss, Mia held her tongue until they were lying in bed. Then, doing her best to recapture her earlier excitement and enthusiasm, she told him about getting the keys to the house.

When it became apparent that he was scarcely listening, unable to stand it any longer, she asked, 'What's the matter? Sander? What's wrong?'

'Why should anything be wrong?'

But she was sure something was. Dreadfully wrong.

He was lying apart from her in the big double bed, his hands clasped behind his head. Though the pose appeared to be a relaxed, indolent one, she knew that in reality he was taut as a drawn bowstring.

For a while now she had followed his example and slept naked. Realising words were useless, she moved to snuggle against him, fitting the length of her body to his. Her lips parted, she used the tip of her tongue to trace the curve of his shoulder, and with a boldness she was just learning, touched him. As her hand brushed lightly over his hipbone and muscular thigh, she felt the jerk of his response. Teasingly she whispered, 'If you won't talk to me, make love to me.'

'Why not?' he said harshly. 'After all, you're still my wife.'

Before she could wonder at his choice of words, he rolled, and, pinning her beneath him, for the very first time took her without any preliminaries, roughly, almost brutally, showing no regard for her at all.

If there was a dark side to him, she was now seeing it, and ought to have been afraid. But something primitive in her responded to the passion she had unleashed. He was her man, her mate, her own dear love. Together they reached a shattering climax.

Afterwards she lay with his head heavy on her breast, one arm holding him, her free hand stroking his crisp dark hair. *Her own dear love*. How foolish she'd been, how incredibly foolish, to have once thought she loved Philip. What she'd felt for him had been like the warmth of a candle flame compared to the white-hot heat of a furnace.

'Oh, God,' Sander muttered after a moment or two. Then, huskily, 'I'm sorry, I never meant to hurt you, my heart's darling.'

Mia caught her breath. 'You didn't . . . You didn't hurt me.' To have him call her 'my heart's darling' in that tone of voice she would willingly have been flayed alive.

When he lifted himself away from her, she nestled against him, and, made brave by his endearment, and wanting his love with every fibre of her being, begged, 'Please, Sander, talk to me. Tell me you love me.'

In the semi-darkness she saw his face tighten with pain before he half turned away.

'Don't shut me out,' she begged. 'At least tell me what's wrong.'

She thought he was about to repulse her again, when he said wearily, 'Very well, I'll tell you. I realise now I made a mistake in marrying you.'

In spite of the warmth she felt icy cold, steel bands around her chest constricting her heart, stopping her breathing. 'A mistake...?' she whispered. 'You mean you should have married Jacqueline May?'

'Of course not. I told you once before, Jacqueline isn't the marrying kind.'

Jealousy, rising bitter as gall, made Mia cry, 'Just the kind who prefers married men?' Instantly ashamed of herself, she mumbled, 'I'm sorry, I shouldn't have said that.'

'No, you shouldn't.' His tone was uncompromising.

Mia bit her lip, then, the words wrenched from her, asked, 'Have you been with her tonight?'

'No.' He sounded surprised. 'I haven't seen her since we had lunch together that day.'

There was no doubt in her mind that he spoke the truth. But now the opportunity had arisen she wanted an answer to the question that had tormented her. 'Sander, why did you take her out to lunch when you wouldn't take me?'

'I felt I owed her that much for old times' sake,' he answered drily. 'She rang me up in tears, said she must see me. Though we had an understanding from the start that, if either of us wanted out, there would be no hard feelings, no recriminations, it seems she wasn't prepared to lose me. She'd returned to London hoping to resume the relationship. Which shows she didn't know me very well. When I told her it really was over, finished, she was . . . upset. If she hadn't been, I would have introduced you.'

Such a wave of relief washed over Mia that she felt faint. 'Then why did you say you'd made a mistake . . .?'

'It was a mistake. I should never have forced you into marrying me.' He sat up abruptly.

Dreadfully afraid, needing to see his face, she followed suit and switched on the light.

There was a pause, then, his voice tightly controlled, he went on, 'I was on the point of leaving the office last night when Rhoda turned up. She was damned near hysterical. She said you'd won after all. Measham had walked out on her after declaring it was you he wanted and the wedding was definitely off.'

'But——'

'I made up my mind it was high time to have it out with him.'

Mia shivered involuntarily.

Feeling the movement, Sander admitted, 'Yes, my first impulse was a primitive urge to break his neck.' A note of self-mockery in his voice, he went on, 'But I decided to try and be civilised about things, so today I called him and suggested we had dinner together.

'I didn't think he'd have the guts to meet me face to face, but to my surprise he agreed to join me at the Meridian.'

'Oh, Sander, you didn't . . . you haven't . . . ?'

'I haven't laid so much as a finger on him,' Sander assured her—adding, cruelly derisive, 'There's no need to sound as concerned as a mother hen whose chick is threatened!'

She had been concerned, not so much about Philip, but about the possible repercussions if Sander had lost his temper.

'I'd chosen a public place so I wouldn't be tempted to half kill him,' Sander continued after a moment. 'Though I did intend to put the fear of God into him.

'When I got there he was waiting for me and we talked. He agreed that there'd been a terrific bust-up and he'd finished with Rhoda for good.'

'Finished with her?' Mia echoed stupidly. 'How can he be finished with her when she's expecting his child?'

'That's one of the things he wants to tell you about.'

'I don't know why he wants to tell me,' Mia protested faintly.

'Because you're the woman he really loves and needs—his words, not mine. He admitted that he can't get through to you, that you won't see him or listen to him, but all the same he's quite certain you still love him.'

'But I don't——'

As though he hadn't heard her, Sander continued, 'He told me how shocked you were when you found out Rhoda and he had been lovers, and he believes you only married me to get even with him. He's also convinced that, now you've committed yourself, you'll ruin both his life and your own rather than be disloyal to me.'

Ignoring Mia's attempt to interrupt, Sander went on, 'In a way I was forced to admire him. Though Measham was obviously shaking in his shoes, he laid it on the line. He thinks that, no matter how unhappy you are, you won't take the initiative and leave me, so he wants me to give you up. He's banking on the fact that now I know the score my pride won't allow me to force a woman who doesn't love me, to stay with me.'

'Sander, I——'

As though too restless to remain still any longer, with one lithe movement he pushed himself up and sat on the edge of the bed. His broad back was to her, and she could see the unmistakable tension in his neck and shoulders and the length of his spine.

Speaking with difficulty now, he said, 'So I'm prepared to give you your freedom. Go to him if you want to, and I'll see you have grounds for a divorce as soon as possible.'

'I . . . I don't want a divorce,' Mia stammered.

Sander drew a deep, harsh breath. 'You love him. God knows you've told me so often enough, and, that day in the summer-house, you were terrified I'd hurt him. Well, he's right. I've decided I don't want a wife who loves another man and who stays with me just out of loyalty.'

'But it's not just out of loyalty! I . . .' Mia stopped abruptly. With Sander in his present mood, this wasn't the time to try and convince him she loved him.

'Besides,' he went on relentlessly, 'the two reasons I had for marrying you no longer apply. Whatever happens, I can't *force* Measham to marry Rhoda, and now control of the bank is in my hands I don't need a wife.'

The words stung, as Mia felt sure they were meant to. Taking a chance, she said daringly, 'You never did need a wife for that reason. You lied about having to be married.'

Turning to face her, he demanded, 'And why would I do that?'

Fighting now for her happiness, she declared, 'Because I was hardly likely to believe you'd tie yourself to me just for Rhoda's sake. You *wanted* to marry me, but to save your pride you needed a more pressing reason. If what you felt for me had been just a physical attraction, you would only have wanted me as a mistress.'

A quick glance showed that his dark face was devoid of expression. With less certainty she went on, 'You didn't want to admit you cared because you thought I loved Philip.'

'That's where you're mistaken,' Sander denied shortly. 'At that stage in the game I couldn't believe that what you felt for Measham *was* love. Then you told me about your childhood, and I thought I'd got the answer. You'd fooled yourself into thinking you cared for him because you *needed* to love and to be loved.' Flatly he added, 'It wasn't until our honeymoon was almost over that I realised I'd been wrong.'

'But you weren't wrong,' she said quietly. 'That's exactly how it was. What little I felt for Philip was more like gratitude.' Then, more forcefully, 'I didn't love him then, I don't love him now, and I don't want a divorce.'

'Measham was right. Your loyalty does you credit.'

'Loyalty, my foot!' she cried.

His dark face implacable, Sander said wearily, 'I realise that by letting your father off the hook, as you put it, I've made you feel indebted to me, made it more difficult for you to leave me for Measham——'

Her indignation rising, Mia stormed, 'This has absolutely nothing to do with feeling indebted to you. I've told you, I've no desire to end our marriage.' Desperately she added, 'I don't understand you at all. It's almost as if you *want* me to go.'

Coldly he said, 'I do.'

Just for a moment her confidence wavered, then it was back full force. 'Only because you're too stubborn to listen to what I'm trying to tell you. *I don't want to leave you*. And even if you threw me out, do you think for one moment that I'd go to *him* when Rhoda's pregnant?'

His green eyes hard, his mouth a thin, straight line, Sander shook his head. 'You don't know the full facts. I suggest you speak to Measham before you finally make up your mind.'

Pulling on his short robe, Sander headed for the door, closing it behind him with a decisive click.

For a moment Mia was tempted to follow him, but what was the use? she thought hopelessly. Trying to convince him was like trying to push Everest over with one hand.

Switching off the light, she lay down again and shut her eyes tightly, but hot tears forced themselves beneath her closed lids and ran down her face in a steady, silent stream. She cried for a long time, needing the release that tears brought.

Throughout a seemingly endless night, alone in the big bed, she tossed and turned, waking repeatedly. Each time she drifted into sleep she dreamt that, despite all her pleas, Sander rejected her. It was almost daylight before she finally fell into a deep slumber.

She opened heavy eyes to find it was practically eleven o'clock, and the whole place seemed silent and deserted.

Feeling anxious and headachy, she showered and pulled on a cream skirt and top before going downstairs. Opening the living-room door, she looked in. The usual cheerful fire was burning in the grate, but the room was empty.

Sander was in the kitchen. Dressed in casual trousers and an open-necked shirt, he was sitting at the breakfast bar, staring into space, a cold cup of coffee in front of him, Saturday morning's paper lying there still folded.

She came silently, in stockinged feet, and surprised such a look of bleak desolation on his strong face that she wanted to weep.

Biting her lip, she plugged in the percolator and got out fresh cups. Neither of them spoke.

Mia had poured the coffee and was drinking hers when the phone rang. Sander lifted his head and looked at her. With a sense of fatalism she picked up the receiver.

'Mia?' It was Philip's voice, as she had known it would be. 'Darling, I've got to talk to you. Will you have lunch with me?'

She didn't want to talk to him, but, remembering Sander's insistence that she should, she agreed shortly, 'All right. Where?'

'The Cleveland.' He sounded tense and agitated. 'I'll wait for you in the restaurant.'

'Very well . . . I'll be there in about half an hour.' She replaced the phone. 'That was Philip. He wants me to have lunch with him.'

All Sander said was, 'Yes.'

The look of anguish in his eyes made her heart feel as if it was being squeezed by a giant fist. 'If you'd rather I didn't go after all?'

He shook his head. 'I want you to go and talk to him, to know your own mind.'

Moving to stand by the window, he looked out across the wet garden, where a blackbird was pouring forth a melodious song. Without turning round, he said, 'If you decide to stay with him, I'd prefer you not to come back. Just let me know where to send your things.'

'Sander,' she began hesitantly, 'if you love me——'

'I don't love you,' he denied harshly.

Her face full of delicate strength, Mia lifted her chin and went to find her bag and outdoor things. On an impulse she picked up the dragon pendant from the dressing-table and, having fastened it around her neck, left without another word.

Philip was waiting in the discreet luxury of the Cleveland's restaurant and rose to his feet at her approach. He was dressed in a blue suit and toning shirt and tie, his shoes polished, his blond hair almost too carefully styled.

'Darling...' he seized both her hands in evident relief '... I still wasn't sure you'd come.'

Though it was only a matter of weeks, he looked older than when she'd last seen him. His pale blue eyes lacked sparkle and, after Sander's magnificent physique, he appeared effete.

Freeing her hands, Mia allowed an attentive waiter to pull out her chair.

When she was seated, Philip sat down opposite and ordered sherry for them both. While he perused the menu she studied him dispassionately, seeing clearly for the first time the petulant curve of his mouth, the weakness of his chin, how his face as a whole lacked strength. Yet he'd managed to stand up to Sander at his most formidable.

Glancing up, Philip asked, 'What would you like to eat?'

'I don't mind,' she said. 'Whatever you're having.'

Plainly disconcerted by her manner, he gave the order.

They sipped their sherry without speaking until the sole *bonne femme* arrived and the wine waiter had poured the chilled Chablis and departed. Then, anxious to get things over, Mia said, 'I understand you've been talking to Sander.'

'So he told you?'

'Yes, he told me.' Almost wonderingly she added, 'You took a big risk meeting him like that.'

'He could hardly beat me up in such a public place,' Philip pointed out. 'And I thought it was worth the gamble. Is he prepared to let you go without a fuss?'

'He's prepared to let me leave him if I want to,' she answered levelly.

'I was sure his pride wouldn't allow him to hold a woman he knew didn't want him,' Philip said with a smile of satisfaction.

'But I do want him.'

He looked momentarily startled, then he said almost accusingly, 'You love me.'

Mia poked at the creamy fish with the prongs of her fork and admitted slowly, 'I once thought I did.'

'You did, and you still do.' Philip looked decidedly peevish. 'But, because you're married to Davison, you won't admit it. You always had too many scruples. You would never let me make love to you because of Rhoda.'

Mia bit her tongue and said, 'Why did you tell Sander the wedding was off?'

'Because it is. Ever since you were married things have gone from bad to worse. She got the idea that you'd only married Davison so we could have an affair on the side. Afterwards we had the worst quarrel we've ever had. I've stood enough of her jealousy, and——'

'But you can't leave her in the lurch when she's having your child!'

'That's just it,' Philip said. 'She isn't.'

'She isn't having a baby?' Mia echoed. 'When did she tell you?'

'She didn't tell me.'

'How did you find out?'

It wasn't the question he'd anticipated, and his handsome face flushing, he muttered, 'How would you expect?'

He looked so guilty that Mia almost smiled. After a moment she asked, 'What went wrong?'

'Nothing went wrong. She never had been pregnant. She'd lied to me. And that alters everything.'

It didn't alter the fact that Philip had been Rhoda's lover, Mia thought. Aloud she said, 'How can you be sure she lied to you? It might have been a genuine mistake.'

'It wasn't a mistake,' he denied shortly. 'When I demanded the truth, she admitted she'd made the whole thing up after she'd found out about us. She said she was afraid I was planning to end the engagement and she'd only done it to keep me——'

'But I don't see how——'

'Apparently she'd intended to *get* pregnant as soon as she could . . .' Looking wounded, he added, 'Even Davison admitted it was a damned dirty trick.'

So that was what Sander had meant when he'd said she didn't know all the facts. But knowing them didn't make any difference to her feelings. Clearly he'd expected her to blame his cousin bitterly, but, though Mia couldn't condone what the other woman had done, in an odd sort of way she felt she owed Rhoda a big debt of gratitude.

Taking a sip of her wine, Mia sighed.

It was a moment or two before she realised that Philip was staring at her nonplussed, obviously having expected a much stronger reaction.

She found herself smiling at his bewilderment.

'I don't see anything funny in being lied to and made a fool of,' he complained bitterly. 'After all, if she hadn't found out about us——'

'I'm sorry,' Mia broke in, adding hastily, 'How *did* she find out, have you any idea?'

Side-tracked, he said, 'You know Miss Hemsley...?'

Recalling the middle-aged, stern-faced woman who was secretary to Rayfield's export manager, Mia nodded.

'Well, it seems she has an elderly widowed sister who she visits a couple of times a week. On her way there she passes your flat. On more than one occasion she noticed my car parked close by, and once she actually saw me coming out.

'She's not a woman to gossip, or it would have been all over the offices. But she did tell her sister, who mentioned it to her daughter who works in the hairdressing salon that Rhoda goes to...'

Philip smoothed a hand over his fair hair and went on, 'I was so angry when I found she'd made a fool of me that I told her everything was over. She turned really nasty then and threatened that, if I left her, in a month I'd be on the end of a dole queue.

'But this time she'd miscalculated. Even her father was shocked that she'd stoop to such a shabby trick and he refused point-blank to sack me, so at least I've still got a job...

'Darling...' reaching across the table, he took Mia's hand '...you know how much I love you. Leave Davison and we'll live together until you can get a divorce.'

'I don't want to leave him, and I don't want a divorce.'

Philip scowled. 'I admit I'm not filthy rich as he is, but I never thought you cared that much about money.'

'It has absolutely nothing to do with money. When I made my marriage vows I intended to keep them.' She pulled her hand away.

'Things have altered,' he protested. 'I'm free now.'

'But I'm not.'

'You can't stay with him just out of loyalty.'

'It isn't just out of loyalty. I'll be staying with him because he's my husband and I love him.'

'I don't believe it,' Philip objected. Then, thickly, 'Does he love you? He may *want* you, but surely he wouldn't be prepared to let you go so easily if he loved you?'

'He loves me,' Mia answered with absolute certainty. 'He loves me enough to care more about my happiness than his own.'

'But you're *my* happiness, and you always said you loved me.' Philip managed to sound like a snivelling small boy.

Mia sighed, and said gently, 'If we'd never met you'd have been happy with Rhoda. I'm sorry, dreadfully sorry, that I've upset things.'

Leaving her meal untouched, she rose to her feet and picked up her bag. 'I hope you'll forget about me and go back to Rhoda. She must love you a lot, otherwise she wouldn't have tried so hard to keep you. Go on, make it up with her. Take her to bed and get her pregnant.'

Philip looked startled, almost shocked.

Impishly, Mia added, 'If you want to keep everything respectable you could marry her first.' Then, more seriously, 'Things will work out if you want them to. Try and be happy. I'm going to be.'

Without looking back, she hurried out of the hotel. The drizzle had stopped and the sun was playing hide-and-seek behind the clouds while it made up its mind whether or not to shine.

She flagged down a taxi and, feeling unable to get back fast enough, asked the driver to hurry. When they reached Crombie Square, she paid him, thrust a generous tip into his hand, and sped up the steps.

Everywhere was so silent that at first she thought Sander had gone out, then through the half-open kitchen door she saw he was still standing by the window, as if he hadn't moved since she'd left.

At the click of the door closing, he turned slowly. She went up to him, put her arms around his neck, and, standing on tiptoe, kissed him on the lips. For an endless moment he stood there as if turned to stone, then his arms closed around her and he returned her kiss with a hunger and need that went too deep for words.

Shaken by emotion so strong that it completely overwhelmed them, they stood for a long time silently embracing, Sander cradling her head to his chest, his mouth muffled in her silky hair.

After a while, wanting to see his face, she drew away a little and, smiling, touched his cheek.

At first he didn't speak, as if afraid to trust his voice, then, taking her hand, he kissed the palm and said softly, 'Well, if you've decided to stay with me, there's a house we should go and look at.'

Tall Trees, with its creeper-clad walls, its crooked chimneys and mullioned windows, was everything Mia had hoped for. Full of mellow light, birdsong, and the scent of may, it had that indefinable atmosphere of contentment that happy houses had.

That night, lying in bed close beside Sander, Mia sighed. 'Isn't Tall Trees the loveliest place you've ever seen? If we paint the kitchen white and primrose and——'

He stopped the rest of the words with a kiss. When his mouth left hers to wander over the silken warmth of her throat and shoulders, she asked dreamily, 'Do you think you could fix up a swing in that big old apple tree for when we have children...?'

'Woman,' he said on a note between passion and laughter, 'if you don't give more attention to fundamental things there won't *be* any children.'

Later, lying in his arms, tracing his firm mouth with one fingertip, a thought occurred to her. 'Sander...can I ask you something?'

'Ask away,' he murmured, lazily content.

'Did you and Rhoda ever have an affair?'

'Good lord, no,' he answered unhesitatingly. 'What gave you that idea?'

'Dad mentioned that she'd once...liked you a lot.'

Sander grunted. 'I've always felt a bit guilty about that, though I did nothing to encourage her... *You* are the only woman whose love I've ever wanted.'

She turned her head to kiss his chin. 'I couldn't tell you this last night, because I was afraid you wouldn't believe me, but I do love you. You're in my heart, in my head, in my blood. If I never saw you again I'd love you while there was breath in my body.'

With an inarticulate murmur he gathered her close, and his kiss claimed her as if she was all he would ever want or need from life.

'It took me a while to realise it,' she went on when finally he freed her mouth, 'and then I couldn't tell you because——'

'Because of what I'd said about having three objectives?'

She nodded. 'I thought it would be safer if I let you go on believing I loved Philip.'

'I should never have rushed you in the way I did. But from the first moment I saw you I wanted you to be mine body and soul.'

'Yet you had such a low opinion of me.'

'Only at first. It was a shock to find out about Measham, and I was angry to think that you weren't as innocent as you looked. You see, I'd been waiting all my life for a woman like you.' His hand curved round her breast and squeezed gently. 'Satisfied?'

'Why?' she asked, with wide-eyed innocence. 'Surely you can't manage it again so soon?'

She gave a squeal as he grabbed her and, growling deep in his throat, proceeded to prove just how wrong she was.

He still hadn't said he loved her, she thought, when he drew her against him and settled her head on his shoulder. But somehow it no longer really mattered. She knew he did, and she was content. All the same...

'Sander...' she let her fingertips roam over his chest, tugging at the short, crisp curls, '...you've never told me you love me.'

He kissed her with a heady combination of tenderness and passion. 'You know how I feel about you.'

She curled her small hand into a fist and thumped him. 'You still haven't said it.'

Picking up the faint trace of disappointment in her voice, he kissed her again and promised, 'Before too long I have it in mind to take you back to Hong Kong to do a spot of kite-flying.'

'OU **CAN** AFFORD THAT HOLIDAY!

eat savings can be made when you book your next holiday – whether you want
go skiing, take a luxury cruise, or lie in the Mediterranean sun – the Holiday
ub offers you the chance to receive **FREE HOLIDAY SPENDING MONEY** worth
to 10% of the cost of your holiday!

you have to do is choose a holiday from one of the major holiday companies
cluding Thomson, Cosmos, Horizon, Cunard, Kuoni, Jetsave and many more.

st call us* and ask if the holiday company you wish to book with is included.

HOW MUCH SPENDING MONEY WILL I RECEIVE?

e amount you receive is based on the basic price of your holiday. Add up the
al cost for all holiday-makers listed on your booking form – excluding
rcharges, supplements, insurance, car hire or special excursions where these
e not included in the basic cost, and after any special reductions which may be
ered on the holiday – then compare the total with the price bands below:-

YOUR TOTAL BASIC HOLIDAY PRICE FOR ALL PASSENGERS	*FREE* HOLIDAY SPENDING MONEY
£ 200...............449	£ 20
450...............649	30
650...............849	40
850...............1099	60
1100...............1499	80
1500...............1999	110 ...
... 8500 or more	500

aving paid the balance of your holiday 10 weeks prior to travelling, your **FREE
OLIDAY SPENDING MONEY** will be sent to you with your tickets in the form of
cheque from the Holiday Club approximately 7-10 days before departure.

e reserve the right to decline any booking at our discretion. All holidays are
bject to availability and the terms and conditions of the tour operators.

HOW TO BOOK

CHOOSE YOUR HOLIDAY from one of
the major holiday companies brochures,
making a note of the flight and hotel
codes.

PHONE IT THROUGH* with your credit
card details for the deposit and
insurance premium, or full payment if
within 10 weeks of departure and quote
P&M Ref: H&C/MBC185. Your holiday
must be booked with the Holiday Club
before 30.6.92 and taken before
31.12.93.

SEND THE BOOKING FORM from the
brochure to the address above, marking
the top right hand corner of the booking
form with P&M Ref: H&C/MBC185.

you prefer to book by post or wish to pay
e deposit by cheque, omit stage 2 and
mply mail your booking to us. We will
ntact you if your holiday is not available.

Send to: The Holiday Club
P O Box 155 Leicester LE1 9GZ
* Tel No. (0533) 513377
Mon – Fri 9 am – 8 pm, Sat 9 am – 4 pm
Sun and Bank Holidays 10 am – 4 pm

CONDITION OF OFFER

Most people like to take out holiday
insurance to cover for loss of possessions or
injury. It is a condition of the offer that
Page & Moy will arrange suitable insurance
for you – further details are available on
request. In order to provide comprehensive
cover insurance will become payable upon
confirmation of your holiday.

Free Holiday Spending Money is not payable
if travel on the holiday does not take place.

The Holiday Club is run by Page & Moy Ltd,
Britain's largest single location travel agency
and a long standing member of ABTA.

N.B. Any contractual arrangements are
between yourselves and the tour operators
not Mills & Boon Ltd.

ABTA 99529 Page & Moy Ltd Reg No. 1151142

WIN A LUXURY CRUISE

TO THE MEDITERRANEAN
AND BLACK SEA

Ever dreamed of lazing away the days on the open sea with all you need to enjoy yourself close at hand, and spending busy, exciting hours ashore exploring romantic old cities and ports?

Imagine gliding across calm blue waters with the sun overhead in a vast blue sky, and waking up in faraway places for breakfast, such as Lisbon with its fashionable shops, or at the famous rock of Gibraltar.

Imagine sailing through the Mediterranean and stopping at Sicily with towering Mt Etna, then arriving effortlessly in Athens with all its many treasures and finally cruising along the Bosphorus and exploring the exotic city of Istanbul.

This experience of a lifetime could be yours, all you need to do is save the red token from the back of this book and collect a blue token from any Mills & Boon Romance featuring the holiday competition in December. Complete the competition entry form and send it in together with the tokens.

Don't miss this opportunity!
Watch out for the Competition
in next month's books

Next month's Romances

Each month, you can choose from a world of variety in romance with Mills & Boon. These are the new titles to look out for next month.

THE STONE PRINCESS Robyn Donald

TWO-FACED WOMAN Roberta Leigh

DIAMOND FIRE Anne Mather

THE GOLDEN GREEK Sally Wentworth

SAFETY IN NUMBERS Sandra Field

LEADER OF THE PACK Catherine George

LOVEABLE KATIE LOVEWELL Emma Goldrick

THE TROUBLE WITH LOVE Jessica Hart

A STRANGER'S TRUST Emma Richmond

HIS WOMAN Jessica Steele

SILVER LADY Mary Lyons

RELUCTANT MISTRESS Natalie Fox

SHADOW HEART Cathy Williams

DEVON'S DESIRE Quinn Wilder

TIRED OF KISSING Annabel Murray

WIFE TO CHARLES Sophie Weston

STARSIGN
STARS IN THEIR EYES Lynn Jacobs

Available from Boots, Martins, John Menzies, W.H. Smith and other paperback stockists.

Also available from Mills and Boon Reader Service, P.O. Box 236, Thornton Road, Croydon, Surrey CR9 3RU.